KARMESIN

KARMESIN
World's Greatest Criminal--
or Most Outrageous Liar

GERALD KERSH
Edited by Paul Duncan

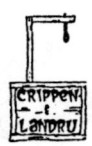

Crippen & Landru Publishers
Norfolk, Virginia
2003

Copyright © 2003 by Gerald Kersh and New Worlds Publishing

Published by permission of New Worlds Publishing, POB 1230, Bastrop, TX 78602

Introduction © 2003 by Paul Duncan (kershed@aol.com)

Back cover photo of Gerald Kersh © 1965 by Simon Richard Bloom

Cover painting by Carol Heyer

"Lost Classics" cover design by Deborah Miller

Crippen & Landru logo by Eric Greene

ISBN (cloth edition): 1-932009-02-7
ISBN (trade edition): 1-932009-03-5

Crippen & Landru Publishers
P.O. Box 9315
Norfolk, VA 23505
USA

www.crippenlandru.com
Info@crippenlandru.com

Contents

Introduction	7
Karmesin	15
Karmesin and the Meter	21
Karmesin and Human Vanity	27
Karmesin and the Tailor's Dummy	35
Karmesin and the Big Flea	43
Karmesin and the Raving Lunatic	51
Karmesin and the Unbeliever	57
Inscrutable Providence	65
Karmesin and the Invisible Millionaire	73
Karmesin and the Gorgeous Robes	81
Chickenfeed for Karmesin	89
The Thief Who Played Dead	97
The Conscience of Karmesin	109
Karmesin and the Royalties	117
Skate's Eyeball	123
Oalámaóa	137
The Karmesin Affair	151
Bibliography	165

Dedication, for Simon Richard Bloom

Your uncle Gerard always said that he'd dedicate one of his books to you. Well, it's a little late, but here it is.

Introduction: Man of Many Skins

The early 1930s were the 'lost' years of Gerald Kersh. Although he considered himself a great writer, he could not sustain himself on the meagre pile of coins and notes that he received from various publishers, magazines and newspapers for whom he contributed novels, short stories and short pieces to fill column inches. For the later, an editor on deadline would call the copy boy and send him around the multitudinous watering holes that peppered Fleet Street and Soho until he had unearthed Kersh. Summoned in various states of inebriation, Kersh would dutifully sit at the typewriter, look at the inches he had to fill, then commence typing. Quickly, without a mistake, Kersh would perform a little miracle — an opinion piece calculated to incite outrage, a strange fact designed to titillate, a poem that would melt the heart or an interesting anecdote that would induce a fit of laughter upon the reader — of precisely the correct length and tone. After collecting his payment, Kersh would disappear into a nearby pub, bar or club.

When the financial strain was too much to bear or, more usually, when his conscience would not allow his malaise to continue, Kersh took whatever work he could get. He was at various times a salesman, a French teacher (he had spent a year in Paris as a teenager) and a bouncer. For this last post he was employed to keep troublemakers like himself out of nightclubs. Yes, Kersh was trouble. He had intellect, knowledge and an ambition to write but they had no real outlet. He was straining at the leash. Physically powerful and emotionally explosive, it was not uncommon for him to be sparked off by the uncouth behaviour of men towards their female partners. Chairs would fly. Knives would be drawn. Marble tables would be dropped on his head. Scars littered his body, evidence of the number of times his had defended the honour of the gentler sex.

All this is by way of introduction, to give you an idea of the milieu that Kersh inhabited, of the fruitless life that he led in the early part of the 1930s. He had just turned twenty and was unformed. He knew nothing of life and he believed, as Ernest Hemingway had stated, that you can only write about what you know. The seedy bars and jazz joints that he habituated were his offices. The cafés and brassieres were his kitchens. The parks and bridges were his bedrooms. He packed a lifetime of experience into a few short years and used it to fuel his subsequent novels and short stories. The most famous of his London novels was *Night and the City* (1938), the story of an idealistic pimp who has plans to be a great man but is doomed to failure, but he also wrote the nihilistic noir thriller *Prelude to a Certain Midnight* (1947) and the hilarious *Fowlers End* (1957). All of them contained elements from his life.

Despite the eventual success of his novels, Kersh is best known for his short stories. Many of them are horrific or fantastical in nature, showing the best and worst in people, but all of them tap into the almost limitless supply of 'characters' that Kersh met over the years. He often presented these stories as himself, as though he was some kind of reporter, and then let these strange characters narrate the rest of the story themselves. This storytelling device gives a touch of veracity to the tales but the reader knows that these are just tales, that they never really happened.

Well, actually, there is a chance that some of them are partly true. Take the Karmesin stories, for example, which are collected here for the first time.

Karmesin (pronounced carr – muh – zin), a name derived from some middle–European term for crimson, is the most sustained character in Kersh's writing career, spanning 17 stories. The first Karmesin story, called simply 'Karmesin,' was published in the London *Evening Standard* on May 9, 1936 whilst the last one, 'The Karmesin Affair,' was published in *The Saturday Evening Post* on December 15, 1962.

Generally, Kersh would meet Karmesin, a middle–aged man with a big moustache, who would proceed to tell tales about his extraordinary criminal exploits. They are so outrageous that they cannot be true, but they are full of seemingly real information about criminals, their methods and perhaps a little about human nature. We begin to doubt Karmesin's stories when we see the way he always asks for cigarettes from Kersh, or surreptitiously stuffs sugar into his pockets. The contradictions in the character are what make him interesting and one would consider

Karmesin an enchanting creation if it wasn't for the fact that he existed in real life.

In letters, Kersh refers to a man named Carfax who was the basis for Karmesin. He told Kersh about a robbery he planned and executed at the Strand branch of Lloyd's bank in which five men simultaneously cashed five large cheques at a great horseshoe shaped counter and walked out. The trick worked only because of the split-second timing of the transactions. This was the basis of the first Karmesin story.

A later story, 'The Conscience of Karmesin,' concerns the robbery of the Crown Jewels from the Tower of London, which Carfax planned. According to Kersh:

> [Carfax] had his technicians examine all the electric wiring leading into the jewel room of the Tower of London, and then rehearsed the robbery in all but its ultimate details over a period of two years. That split-second timing, which characterised the great ghost train mail robbery, he works out himself. He owns custom-made stopwatches that cost £5,000 each. He has a staff of watchmakers in Geneva. So he stole the crown jewels, or was about to do so when purely sentimental considerations made him call the job off.
>
> King George VI you know had a very bad stutter. His wife, Queen Elizabeth, secretly held his hand when he had to make a speech giving it an affectionate little squeeze when she sensed a stutter coming along. Now when King George VI and Queen Elizabeth visited New York he was told of a night school up in Harlem for people who stammered. He was very interested in it. Flossie [Kersh's wife] and I had a servant named Kitty Hinton, a negress, a sort of female Jeeves, a copper-coloured Admiral Crichton, very beautiful what is more, but a stutterer. Being the brightest girl in the class, she was told that she would be required to make a speech to a foreign visitor and give him a little bouquet of flowers. On the appointed evening a little fellow of no great distinction turned up and told them of his lifelong battle against his vocal impediment and how he had, with his wife's help, got the

better of it. Applause. Our Kitty comes forward with a bunch of flowers, loses her nerve at the last moment and stutters like a light machine gun. The visitor held her hand, told her to look at him, and to her amazement she got through the whole speech without pause or error. Later she learned that this quiet little gentleman was the King of England, who would come uptown unescorted, without a single bodyguard, to talk incognito to the likes of Kitty. I wrote this story, but it was never published "for fear it might offend minority sensibilities."

One night, meeting Carfax in a hotel in Northiam, between Kent and Sussex, over a Skate's Eyeball, or let us say, side-stepping the blast of the one who was splashing his way through ... I happened to tell him this anecdote. It brought tears to his eyes. As a child he had been a stutterer and had continued to be one until cured at the age of fourteen by being beaten almost to death and thrown into the Thames below Limehouse in the dead of Winter. I little knew that my idle chatter saved the Crown and the Orb and the Sceptre too, among other things. For Carfax, as he told me later, at once went out and cancelled the Tower job. Two of his men went on with it, against his orders. What happened to them nobody knows — we'll find out when the sea gives up its dead no doubt. They pulled the robbery though. Carfax sent the loot back untouched, he swears. That sort of thing doesn't get into the papers of course.

Immediately after Karmesin's first appearance, Kersh was keen to sell more stories and to exploit other media like radio. On July 3, 1936, Kersh submitted three Karmesin stories to Felix Felton at the BBC, but Felton was not interested. However, Kersh struck lucky with publisher Norman Kark, who was the first to publish 10 of the Karmesin stories in the upmarket *Courier* magazine, starting with the first issue in 1937. Such was their popularity, that Kersh was inundated with offers:

Introduction

[Karmesin] came near to making my life a misery in the late 1930s — editors kept asking for him. I practically got stuck with him the way Simenon got stuck with Maigret — a character with which poor Georges has been heartily fed up with these 20 years or more. You should have heard him cutting off a strip about it on Anna Maria Key in Florida. I did — we were neighbours.

During World War Two, Kersh wrote several million words of propaganda material for the national newspapers and was the best-selling author in the UK with his novels and short story collections being published every six months. In 1945 he used a trip to America for the Ministry of Information to make contacts with magazine editors and this began his relationship with *Ellery Queen's Mystery Magazine*, who reprinted the Karmesin stories. Obviously encouraged by Karmesin's popularity in America, Kersh wrote a few new stories and then dropped the character again.

The character stayed alive in many people's eyes because the stories were reprinted in magazines under a multitude of titles. It is a bibliographic nightmare trying to keep track of them all. The alternative titles were obviously an attempt to hide the origins of the stories, but Kersh didn't help matters by always giving editors a choice of titles. For example, when he delivered 'Chickenfeed for Karmesin,' Kersh also suggested it could be called 'A Snip for Karmesin,' 'Karmesin and the Odds on Underselling' and 'The Value of Self-Denial,' but *Ellery Queen's Mystery Magazine* decided to call it simply 'Karmesin the Fixer.'

Such was the success of the appearances in *Ellery Queen's Mystery Magazine* that they asked for more in 1955 and Kersh began work on a story that pitted the fictional Karmesin against the all-too-real Carfax. This perhaps reflected Kersh's uneasiness with Karmesin:

> If I invented Karmesin nowadays, I don't know but that I'd make him Carfaxian in type, a kind of uniquely contradictory pastiche, very oniony, very salty, highly cheesey and juniperous, and either a fat boiled beef and pease pudding and squeezed out cabbage standing up at a shelf in the steam of a cookhouse

> where there is one napkin to every eight customers and the forks are chained down, where you order by the ounce and watch the stuff being weighed too. (I once saw [Carfax] eat 36 ounces of boiled mutton with onion sauce in Shortlands, and once at the establishment of Harris the sausage king near Paddington eat 14 large sausages — he didn't like 13 — and two soup plates full of onions.)

It seems that the extraordinary and judicious Karmesin was not extraordinary enough or as flamboyant as his real–life counterpart. Despite this, the character had fans all over the world including authors Rex Stout and Henry Miller, philosopher Bertrand Russell, boxer Archie Moore, owner of the Algonquin Hotel Ben Bodne, actor Basil Rathbone, Governor Rockefeller, publishing magnate Lord Beaverbrook and Sir Winston Churchill. Kersh received repeated requests from actors like Walter Slezak, Burl Ives and Sir Cedric Hardwicke (who narrated some of the stories on American radio) to consider them for the role of Karmesin should the opportunity arise on stage or screen. In fact, Kersh began talking to contacts within the TV industry about a possible series. Although scripts were written and actors like Francis L. Sullivan and Charles Laughton considered for the lead, a series was not commissioned. However, Erich von Stroheim played Karmesin in the 1956 TV film *Orient Express: Man of Many Skins*. This was the pilot for a TV series centred around Major North, a character created by Van Wyck Mason. Directed by Steve Sekely and produced by John G. Nasht, the series did not materialise, and neither did Kersh's money for the project.

Three Karmesin stories materialised in the mid–1950s and another three in the early 1960s, perhaps in an effort to generate interest in the character on TV. And that was it for Karmesin. However, Carfax retained a fascination for Kersh and vestiges of him resurfaced occasionally in other characters, most notably as the nemesis in the novel *The Angel and the Cuckoo* (1966). It was not the amorality of the character that interested Kersh but the way in which he applied his intellect and superior knowledge to make money, as shown in this anecdote:

> Another instance of this strange character's unique nose for the valuable: about 4 o'clock one morning I was having

breakfast at Sabini's café in Soho when Carfax/Karmesin came in, bored. He likes me — God knows why. He said, "less take a ball'o'chalk up the cattle market," meaning a walk to the junk market in the Caledonian Road at Pentonville. He wanted fresh air so off we went to that wonderful old market as it was when I was young.

Carfax/Karmesin looked amused whilst I rifled through books. He sniffed at piles of bits of timber, rusty cartwheels and whatnot, and pulled out a most wretched looking bamboo walking stick black with dirt. "Ow much, cock?" he asked the junk man. "A tizzy," the man said, meaning sixpence. "You mean tuppence." So he got the stick for thrupence and gave it to me saying, "Valuable old stick." I took it between thumb and forefinger, not wishing to offend him by refusing.

Meanwhile he had found a huge old tray of baroque design with a tremendous inkstand attached to it, complete with sandbox, waferbox etc. He is a very strong man but even he grunted with the effort of lifting it. "Ow much for this ere?" "Blimey, guy, the lead alone's worth three half crowns." "Don't talk wet you soppy sod, I'll give you a tosheroon." i.e. half crown, two shillings and sixpence. Then about 55 cents. In the end he got the tray for about 80 cents.

It now being six o'clock in the morning we went to Billingsgate market to breathe the aroma of fish and listen to the latest in cursing. In the back parlour of a pub nearby Carfax/Karmesin looked proudly at his purchase. He got a fishmonger's steelyard and weighed it. It tipped the beam at 42lb. I asked, "What the devil do you want a thing like that for?" He took out a penknife and scraped off a square inch of the green paint with which the thing was covered — it was pure gold. Then he remembered something and said, "You owe me thrupence for that stick. Clean it up nice. I'm sure that's a valuable stick." I took it home and cleaned it with soft soap. There was a pattern under the dirt, and what a pattern. The dirt was clean by comparison. From ferrule to band, the bamboo was most exquisitely carved and delicately inlaid in silver with scenes of oriental lovemaking excruciatingly obscene. A great artist must have worked for years on it. I wrapped it in newspaper and sold it to an antiquary for £10.

In 1968, Gerald Kersh died in relative poverty in a shack in Kingston, New York State. He had been cut open and apart by doctors to remove various cancers that had invaded his body. He continued writing right up until the end, reliving his lost years in Soho and putting them down on paper for posterity. I'm happy that at last some of his 'lost' words have been found again and collected here.

Paul Duncan

Karmesin

I never appreciated arithmetical progression, until, in Busto's apartment house, I learned how tea three times infused becomes intolerably weak, and how cigarette-ends twice rolled grow unbearably strong.

I may have learned a little geometry at school, but I had to struggle with Busto's blankets before I realised how ridiculously incongruous two rectangles can be, and I had to sleep on one of Busto's beds before I got to know the difference between looking at an angle and lying on one.

In short, I completed my education in Busto's apartment-house. The physics of cold and darkness became as an open book to me; I picked up zoology without a tutor — I studied it by matchlight, with nothing but a thumbnail for a scalpel; and Karmesin taught me how to rob a bank.

I wish you could have met that powerful personality, that immense, old man with his air of shattered magnificence.

I see again his looming chest and unfathomable abdomen, still excellently dressed in a suit of sound blue serge; the strong cropped skull and the massive purple face.

The tattered white eyebrows and the heavy, yellowish eyes, as large as little plums; the vast Nietzsche moustache, light brown with tobacco-smoke, which lay beneath his nose like a hibernating squirrel, concealing his mouth, and stirring like a living thing as he breathed upon it.

And what was Karmesin? If the things he told me were true he must have been the greatest criminal of his time. If they were not then he must have been the greatest liar of all time. He was one of these two things; which one I have never been able to determine.

"The fact is that I have what you would call a creative mind," said Karmesin.

"A remarkable talent for fiction?" I suggested.

"That is quite right. I have conceived many crime-stories, and then made them come true. There is money to be made out of such fiction. Why are there no detective-story-writers who are successful criminals?

Simply because they are too nervous, and my energy was colossal. But to be a writer it is necessary to be lazy."

"And so you really have committed perfect crimes?"

"I have already said so."

"I've been told that there's no such thing."

"Yes, I know. The little slip that brings the criminal to justice. That was invented by writers. Why *should* one make a little slip? I never did."

"Never?"

"I have never pandered to the traditionalists. I have never been so obliging as to knock cigar-ash all over the floor, or to trample on the flower-beds with peculiar boots. *Pfui!* I once made a slight mis-calculation, but never a slip."

"Then the crime couldn't have been perfect."

"On the contrary, it was. The slight miscalculation had nothing to do with the actual crime, which was quite neat and beautiful.

"But it was a lesson to me. I have kept every documentary evidence of that crime, in order to check any possible excess of exuberance in subsequent moments of triumph."

Karmesin fumbled in an inside pocket and took out an ancient pass-book, dated 1910, stamped with the imprint of Lombard's Bank and inscribed with the name of Ivan Jovanovitch. His fingers flicked over the pages. He pointed to the last entry, indicating a credit balance of over three thousand pounds.

"You will observe, my friend, that a M. Jovanovitch had three thousands pounds to his credit in Lombard's Bank."

"Yes?"

"I was Jovanovitch."

"Your savings?"

"Endeavour not to be stupid. I am now telling you the story of a perfect bank robbery. In a few months one may show a profit of fifteen thousand pounds. It is a profitable side-line."

"Did you work it?"

"Need you ask? I will tell you the procedure. I arrived in England in January 1910. My name, for the time being, was Jovanovitch. My passport said so. I was a merchant, you understand, with excellent references, dealing in Eastern European commodities.

"I took a very good suite of offices in a very good part of the City and settled down to do business."

"And did you really do business?"

"Yes, why not? Do you think that one has to behave in accordance with Sherlock Holmes and other rabble and slink through back alleys with a crafty look on the face? Is it essential to go about like a fictitious financier with cigars and gardenias, *chort vizmi!* and other trinkets?...

"Yes, I imported tobacco from the Balkans. There is good honest profit in Serbian tobacco. I also opened this current account at Lombard's Bank. I deposited three thousand pounds.

"For over six months I carried on my legitimate business. I received cheques from well-known firms and paid them into my account.

"I withdrew sums of money. Sometimes they rose to four thousand. In general, however, I kept a steady cash balance of three thousand pounds — but you must already have guessed my plans?"

"I assure you I haven't the faintest idea."

"Ha! And these are the people that set themselves up as critics! *Ekh!*"

"Well, after six months, what happened?"

"At this point it became necessary to enlist the services of three collaborators. They were men I knew very well; three Hungarians named Lajos, Hundyadi and Kovacs — I do not think that Kovacs was his real name, but that is of no consequence.

"I put my proposition to them. I asked them if they would care to earn — two hundred pounds was a lot of money.

"These men, moreover, were Hungarians. I need scarcely say that they saw eye to eye with me. Then, when everything was ready, I went to Lombard's Bank and asked to see the manager."

Karmesin paused.

"Well?" I said.

"Do you mean to say that you still fail to see my idea?"

"I do."

"And yet it is so childishly simple."

"Well, you went to see the manager ..."

"Yes. You observed on my pass-book that my branch of the bank was the File Street branch, which is one of the busiest branches of

Lombard's Bank. You have, no doubt, seen the inside of it, if only from a distance. It is as large as the main entrance to a big railway station.

"A dozen tellers work at a huge counter, which goes round in a curve, not unlike a race-track. Bear this in mind. Well, as I was saying, I arranged to see the manager, and I met that very busy gentleman in his office.

"I said to him: 'Forgive me if I use a little of your valuable time, but I have a rather unusual request to make.'

" 'What is that, Mr. Jovanovitch?'

" 'I have opened certain negotiations with the firm of Leducet Cie. It is absolutely essential that I keep on good terms with them.'

" 'Yes?'

" 'I have to make a cash payment to them of five thousand pounds.'

" 'Oh, but —'

" 'Oh, don't be alarmed,' I said, 'I know that I have only three thousand pounds at present deposited with you. I have the other two thousand pounds with me now.' And I took from my wallet banknotes to the value of two thousand pounds, and put them on the manager's desk.

"So that brought my credit to a total of five thousand pounds.

"Well, the manager looked at the notes, and then he looked at me, and he said: 'I still don't quite see ...'

" 'My position,' I said, 'is this. It is absolutely essential that I convey to Leduc's agent an impression of financial solidity. I know I have enough to my credit to meet the cheque which they will present for payment on Friday morning. Is that so?'

" 'Of course, Mr. Jovanovitch.'

" 'Well, when their agent presents the cheque I want you to pay him the cash without hesitation. I do not want your clerks to look up my account.

" 'There must be no delay in the payment; no query; nothing at all of that sort. Can you arrange this for me?'

" 'Well, Mr. Jovanovitch, it is a rather unusual request, but I see no reason why not.'

" 'Excellent. I should be very grateful if you would be so kind as to instruct your chief clerk to that effect now, in my presence,' I said. 'You will understand that this means a great deal to me and it would set my mind at rest.'

" 'Why, yes,' the manager said, and he called in the chief clerk and gave him those instructions."

I looked at my boots to avoid Karmesin's searching glance.

"Well?" I said.

"Good God above! Can't you see? At precisely mid-day on Friday, at the busiest hour, I, carefully disguised, together with my three collaborators, each of us with an identical cheque for five thousand pounds, walked up to four clerks at convenient distances along that enormous counter and walked out together with twenty thousand pounds!"

"Magnificent!" I exclaimed.

"Boldness and simplicity were the keynotes of that little effort," said Karmesin with a reminiscent smile.

"And what happened then?"

"Why, in two seconds we were in a motor-car which was waiting outside — *paf, paf!* We were gone. That was a perfect crime."

"But I seem to remember your mentioning something about a miscalculation," I said.

"*Da!* We reached a place a few miles out at which we were to part. I took out three packets of small notes and said: 'Here, boys, two hundred pounds each, as arranged. Now let me have those bank-notes.'

"You may imagine my astonishment when Kovacs took out a heavy revolver ..."

Karmesin shrugged his shoulders so philosophically that a piece of plaster fell down from the ceiling.

"They got away with it?" I asked.

"Even my watch," said Karmesin, "but what can one do? One learns by one's mistakes. All the same it was a pity. Twenty thousand pounds was a lot of money before the war."

And he thrust into the mysterious hinterland of his gargantuan moustache the last of a packet of cheap cigarettes.

Karmesin and the Meter

Bop! went my gas ring and extinguished itself. In permutations and combinations of six adjectives and three nouns, I blasted and I damned the bodies and souls of the Gas Companies. Karmesin was at this moment sitting at my table. He had, in front of him, a tin tobacco box, full of cigarette ends; with his usual deliberation, he quietly extracted the tobacco which he put into a saucer, and threw the torn papers back into the box. He could probably see in the dark. The failure of the gas did not disturb him. As I paused for breath I heard the faint crackling of the tiny pieces of paper and dried tobacco, and the ponderous deliberate voice of Karmesin, demanding in an elephantine mutter: —

"What seems to be upsetting you?"

"The gas," I said, "I haven't got another penny."

"Yes," said Karmesin, "It is irritating how little gas one gets for one's penny. Nevertheless, my young friend, you must learn to be philosophical. Light a candle."

"And how the devil," I said, "can I cook an egg with a candle?"

"Eat it raw," said Karmesin; and crackle! crackle! went another cigarette. "Have you got any cigarette papers?"

"No."

"*Chort vizmi!*" bellowed Karmesin.

"Chew it," I said malignantly, pointing to the tobacco.

"All right," said Karmesin. "Do not imagine that it is so easy to defeat a man like me. When you are my age, my young friend, you will learn a little philosophy. Calm, balance, and a faculty for objective reasoning, these things are necessary in this life —"

... I have mentioned Karmesin; that powerful personality; that immense old man with his air of shattered magnificence. I wish you could have met him — Karmesin, with his looming chest and unfathomable abdomen, still excellently dressed in a suit of sound blue serge; with the strong, cropped skull and the massive purple face; the tattered white eyebrows and the heavy yellowish eyes as large as plums; the vast Nietzsche moustache, light brown with tobacco-smoke, which lay beneath his nose like a hibernating squirrel, concealing his mouth and stirring like a living thing as he breathed upon it — Karmesin the greatest criminal, or the greatest liar of his time ...

"Listen," I said, "Say one cut a piece of cardboard to the size of a penny —"

"No," said Karmesin. "It would be a waste of time. I know a man who tried that once. Not merely did it fail to work, but it also jammed the mechanism of the gas meter; he had to confess to his landlord. To failure was added humiliation. He was a young man like you —"

"Was that one of *your* great fiascos?"

"My friend," said Karmesin, "I do not indulge in fiascos. I have a creative mind, a grasp of facts, and an almost incredible foresight. When I swindle a gas company, it is not for pennies but for thousands of pounds."

"Thousands of pounds?" I asked.

"Well, francs, anyway."

"Do you mean to say you have actually got money out of a gas company?"

"It was simple," said Karmesin. "But then, all truly great crimes are simple. One may always rely upon the ordinary man's inability to see what is obvious. What is a genius? A man with a firm grasp of the obvious, plus a creative touch. Thus, in the winter of 19— when I found myself ill and temporarily short of money in Paris, I discovered a means whereby I could obtain free heating and light, and furthermore get heavily paid for doing so. In cash! 10,000 francs. That put me on my feet. It was with the capital that I obtained from the gas company that I was able to go to Brazil and perpetrate perhaps one of the most artistic diamond robberies of all time —"

Karmesin is, as I have said, quite supreme; if not as a criminal, then as a story teller. It is quite easy to associate that immense, genial, aged, and philosophical man of mystery with almost any kind of lawlessness. He has a way with him. You tend to believe every word that finds its way through his cigarette-stained Nietzsche moustache. You cannot help liking the man. You feel that if you are to be swindled or otherwise taken in, you would rather have Karmesin do it than anybody else. He is this kind of man: if he stole your wallet, you would say, "I'm sorry there's not more in it." But, how could such a man stoop to crime? Or, on the other hand, to lying?

"I never know when to believe you," I said.

"My dear sir," said Karmesin, "I comfort myself with the memory of this incident, whenever the gas fails.

"This is how it was. I found myself in Paris. In all businesses one has one's ups and downs. This was a barren period. It had been necessary for me, on account of certain unforeseen circumstances, to leave Geneva in a great hurry, and to travel in a third–class carriage across France. French third–class carriages even in these times are bad enough, but before the War they were worse. It is scarcely extraordinary, therefore, that I contracted a severe attack of influenza which stretched me on my back in my little room, off the Boulevard Ornano.

"I may say that I carried French papers in the name of Charles Lavoisier. I spoke French like a Parisian. That is nothing. I speak eleven languages like a native, even Finnish.

"You must imagine me therefore lying upon my bed of suffering in this abominable little room in the atrocious cold of one of the severest winters on record. My rent was paid for a quarter in advance, and I had a certain amount of credit with the local tradesmen, but all my portable property was gone. I had no money, and the room was very cold. This is the quality of Parisian blankets; they are of some diaphanous substance lightly sprinkled with fluff; when you cover yourself with them all the fluff flies into your nostrils leaving nothing but a sort of woven basis, so thin that no bug dares to set foot on them for fear of falling through and breaking his legs. Even in the midst of my fever my brain began to work. Picture to yourself one unquenchable spark of genius fighting single–handed against the fogs and the vapours of influenza — that was the brain of Karmesin! Outside, the snow came down, melted and turned to ice. There were nights of appalling frost —"

"Well," I said, "well, what about the gas company?"

"I'm just coming to that. Even in the midst of my fever I had an inspiration. I thought it out overnight and in the morning my gas lights were burning, my gas radiator was glowing and I had stopped shivering; and yet I had achieved this without putting a single coin in the meter and without tampering with its mechanism."

"How did you manage that?"

"Wait! A fortnight passed. The man from the gas company came to empty the meter.

"He read the little dials, saw that so many cubic feet had been consumed, opened the meter and found it empty. He was a French official with an absurd beard.

"He said: — 'M'sieur, your meter is empty.'

"I said: — 'M'sieur the collector, that is nothing to me.'

"He said: — 'But where is the money?'

"I replied: — 'Monsieur, I am a sick man. I cannot sit here and answer your riddles. Have the goodness to go.'

"He said: — 'Monsieur, this will have to be reported.'

"I said: — 'Go to the devil.' He replaced the padlock and sealed it. All the same, I had gas for the next fortnight. Then the collector came again with another official. First of all they examined the seal on the padlock and found it intact; it was one of those complicated lead seals that cannot easily be tampered with. Then they looked at the glaring lights and the red hot stove. Then the inspector gave me one of those looks with which lesser men than myself are so easily terrified, opened the box and found nothing.

"You could have heard the argument as far away as the Place D'Anvers.

"Result? They decided that my meter was faulty, took it away, and replaced it with a new one. A devil of a meter, as large and as red as an omnibus, with a mechanism that made a noise like a lady in a car changing gear.

"A week later they came again, again found all the gas lights burning and a room like an oven. It took them about three-quarters of an hour to open the meter, they had locked it up so tight. And what did they find? Empty space!" roared Karmesin, with a shout of laughter, that made the water jug dance in its basin and the window panes vibrate.

"But, Karmesin," I asked, "*How* did you manage it?"

"Wait," said Karmesin. "That is exactly what the gas people asked me. I simply smiled a mysterious smile and said nothing. And then one day, as I expected, I was politely invited to interview one of the directors of the company, and he said something to this effect: — 'Monsieur Lavoisier, I don't know what you're up to but it certainly can't be legal. What tricks have you been playing with our meter?'

"I merely smiled. 'Come, Monsieur,' said this gas man, 'we wish to be lenient. We do not wish to prosecute. Tell us exactly how you cause these meters to function without putting any money in, and we will let the matter rest — we might even forget about the small item of gas you have consumed without paying for it!'

"I said: 'If I tell you, Monsieur, you will not only refrain from prosecuting but you will also pay me 20,000 francs. If you do not do this then I shall discreetly make public a perfectly simple method whereby the consumers of your gas can get it free of charge. It really is just as well for you to know these things. It would be worth more than 20,000 to you.'

'This is preposterous!' he shouted.

" 'You would have to modify all your meters,' I insinuated.

"We compromised at 10,000, and he went with me back to my room."

"Well?" I asked.

"The whole thing was so simple. I pointed to the bottom of the meter and showed him a tiny hole, no larger than a pinhole. That was number one, then I showed him my cake of soap; apparatus No. 2. 'Well?' asked the gas director. I took him to the window and opened it. Lying in the window sill were two or three cakes of soap; in each cake an indentation of the size of a silver franc.

"It was so childishly simple. Into my little soap moulds I had poured water; the night frost turned the water to ice; the one-franc piece of ice was just hard enough to operate the mechanism of the meter; the gas thus obtained heated the room, the heat turned the ice back to water which dripped out at my little pin hole. Result? Invisibility!"

"That's extraordinarily clever," I said. "And did you get your 10,000 francs?"

"Yes," said Karmesin. "But what the devil was 10,000 francs? £500? £500! Chicken feed! —"

Karmesin rolled some of his twice-used cigarette tobacco into a kind of mahorka-cigarette, in a bit of newspaper, and fumigated his gigantic moustache with a puff of frightfully acrid smoke.

Karmesin and Human Vanity

Karmesin was looking at himself in the mirror. The mirror measured some few square inches. Karmesin's surface measurements must have run to some almost astronomical number of square feet: he had to take four looks to see the whole of his face. He passed a hand over his cropped white head, which gave out a noise such as you might make by rubbing together two pieces of sandpaper; scowled at himself with his ponderous eyebrows, and then, with a deft gesture, divided into two parts his gigantic Nietzsche moustache and gave the ends a twirl; slapped himself in the chest, tried to look at the back of his neck, dragged down his cuffs, polished his shoes on the backs of his trouser-legs, and, in general, indulged in such an orgy of titivation that I could not help asking: —

"Are you going to meet a woman, or something?"

"No. My day is finished. Observe my hair, how white it has gone. Also this moustache. There was a time when no woman could resist this moustache; a certain duchess used to tie little pieces of ribbon to the ends of it. But it is all vanity ..."

"Bits of ribbon!" I said.

Karmesin swung round his big, plum-like eyes, and glared at me. "The trouble with you, my fine fellow," he said, "is that you are a sceptic. You believe nothing that you do not see. Therefore you are a fool. 'Seeing is believing!' *Pfui*, I say; and again, *Pfui!* It is thirty years since I last saw my own knees. So am I therefore to refuse to believe in them? There is no fool quite so foolish as the sceptic, the Wise Guy. *I* know. I know all about fools. So listen to what I say. The greatest blockhead on earth is the clever man who thinks himself cleverer. Hence, I could extract a hundred thousand francs from a man of whom it was said: — 'The banknotes trickle through his fingers like flypapers.' "

"Who was that?"

"A man called Medved, a crook."

"How did you swindle him?"

Karmesin chuckled. "Listen," he said.

"You might have thought," said Karmesin, "that the man was not born who could swindle Medved. There was no under-handed trick that he had not thought of first. He was more slippery than a basinful of eels, and subtle with a fantastic subtlety — almost as subtle as myself.

"There was no dirty business with which he had not soiled his hands. He had dipped his fingers in a thousand different pockets. He was clever, and he knew it. First teach a skunk how to make a smell, then teach Medved a new trick! Ha, it was for Karmesin to do that; yes, *chort vozmi*, me, Karmesin, by heaven!

"He was one of those men who can both get money and keep it. He must have been a millionaire. He kept accounts. He introduced a post-office atmosphere into his shady dealings. Not a stamp, not a pen-nib escaped him, and he would stay up half the night to figure out what had happened to a mislaid farthing. You cannot conceive the caution and the meanness of that man! He would have made a Syrian pawn-broker appear like Diamond Jim Brady. But he had brains, and also nerve. At the same time, he was as smooth as glycerine. He looked like an octopus — he had a dirtyish pallor, no shape, evil eyes, and a beak. In shaking hands with him, you felt that six or seven other hands were investigating your pockets while a dozen eyes watched you. He was feared. He made money out of everything. But he was still unknown to the police.

"I met him in Paris. I was very prosperous at this time. You could have seen me in an overcoat with a sable collar and a stud worth a thousand pounds, looking like a magnate. And it entered my mind that it would be an achievement to separate this Medved from a few of his carefully hidden thousands. I took him to Olsen's Bar, gave him champagne, and let him see that my wallet was packed with beautiful new five-hundred-franc notes. I could feel his wicked eyes crawling all over me.

"After a while he said: — 'You are doing well.' I replied: — 'Very well.' 'And might one ask which branch of business you have decorated with your unquestionable talents, Monsieur Schall?' I smiled, and said, quite openly: — 'Undoubtedly, my dear Monsieur Medved, I shall be very happy to tell you. I have a mint.' He laughed. I took out my wallet, showed him its contents, and selected a five-hundred-franc note, which I threw across the table to him. 'What do you think of that note?' I asked. He was not the man to be deceived by a forgery. He handled the note, held it to the light, and said: — 'I think it's very nice. In fact, genuine. It *is* genuine.' I smiled, and said: — 'And what would you say if I told you that it was not?' 'Why, then,' he replied, 'I should say that you have found a genius of an engraver, a master of printing, and the greatest paper–maker in the world.' I said: — 'You would be wrong. I have found no such things. One genius, yes. But that is neither here nor there. You must excuse me. I have to go.'

" 'Wait,' he said. 'This note: it is certainly genuine.' I replied: — 'Keep it as a souvenir. It is not genuine. Take it into any bank. Tell the cashier: I have every reason to suspect that this note is a forgery. Have it scrutinised. And still they will pronounce it genuine! And still the fact will remain that it was made in a hotel bedroom, in Vienna, with an apparatus not much larger than a typewriter.'

"His heart must have turned over at this, but he simply blinked, and said: — 'We might do business together.' 'Forgive me,' I said, 'but there is no business that I have to discuss with you.' I gave him my card, and left him.

"As I expected, he followed me. He telephoned every day. Once or twice, I took him to dinner, always paying the bill with a new five–hundred–franc note. I let a month pass, six weeks. We talked of everything — except the apparatus not much larger than a typewriter, although his tongue was itching to discuss it. Once I showed him a German hundred–mark note; on another occasion, a new American hundred–dollar bill. To cut it short — in the end, he begged me to tell him about it, and I did.

"The process, as I explained it to him, was simple. I did not involve myself in the innumerable technical complexities of bank–note manufacture. No. I ran no risk of detection through faulty inks or engraving. No. I had, I told him, a method of *transferring the imprint* of a note on to a blank sheet of paper. Hence, I could interleave blank paper and real banknotes, and, within twelve hours, double the number of the notes.

"He asked: — 'And the apparatus?'

"I told him: — 'A sort of metal bath, combined with a heater and press. It is exceedingly simple.' 'May I see it, Monsieur Schall?' 'No, you may not, Monsieur Medved.' 'Did you invent it, Monsieur Schall?' 'No, not entirely. The combination of chemicals essential to the process was invented by an Austrian chemist who works in a dye factory. I helped to elaborate the press. The greatest difficulty is the paper, but I am able to obtain that.' 'And is it a costly process?' he asked. I told him: — 'There is a certain cost. It would cost one about five shillings to duplicate five thousand notes of five-hundred francs each. What more do you want?' He thought for a while, and said: — 'I should like to see such a machine working.' I laughed, and said: — 'I find your company very pleasant, my dear Medved, but I have not yet the honour and pleasure of knowing you well enough for that!' He hastened to assure me. 'My motive is not merely curiosity, Monsieur Schall. If this machine works, I would be prepared to make an offer.' 'No doubt, Monsieur Medved, but I should not be keen to sell.'

"So it went on, for two weeks more. At length, I agreed to give him a demonstration, on the understanding that, if he was satisfied, he would be prepared to buy the press and the formula for two hundred and fifty thousand francs."

Karmesin laughed. I said: — "But Karmesin, you're not going to tell me that you really *could* turn one note into two?"

"Aren't I? You'll see, my friend. I arranged to show Medved what my machine could do. I told him: — 'Have ready at your flat one thousand new notes of a hundred German marks.' He protested: — 'Why German marks?' 'Because the only paper I have is German bank paper, and of that, at present, I have no more than twelve hundred sheets. I'll show you whether this machine works or not! In eight hours, I shall turn one hundred thousand marks into two hundred thousand; in your presence, and before your very eyes.' He said: — 'Very well. Be at my flat at mid-day tomorrow, with your machine, and everything else necessary. The money will be there.'

"Good. Next day, I took my machine, and went to Medved's flat — a grim and filthy place, over a grocer's shop off the Boulevard Rochechouart. I went upstairs. Medved was there, with another fellow, a sort of ape, with a broken face and tremendous shoulders, whose right hand was perpetually in his coat pocket. 'Just in case,' said Medved, very sweetly. 'Not that I distrust you. God forbid. Only nothing could be easier than to knock me down and walk out with my hundred thousand marks.' I said to him: — 'Medved, if I wanted to rob you, the last thing I should stoop to would be robbery with violence. I would swindle you if

I could, yes. But knock you down? *Pfui!*' He said: — 'Let us see the machine.'

"I took it out of its case. It looked like a common black tin box. I opened it and showed Medved the inside. 'Look well,' I said, 'it is very simple. This is a sort of tank of thick glass. This top plate is simply a press, to hold the contents down firmly. Here, as you see, is a spirit–lamp, which heats the surrounding water–jacket. The entire secret of the process is in the compound which transfers the imprint of the real note to the blank paper, and with which we thoroughly moisten every note and every blank sheet before putting them into the press. I will show you, now ...'

"I picked up the bundle of bank–notes, and examined them, one by one. Medved's ape–man watched me so closely that his breath tickled my neck. Medved, also, was all eyes. They thought that I might perform some trick of legerdemain, and palm a few notes. Fools! Fools, to rest so confident in their own knowledge of low crime!

"I damped every note and every sheet of paper, and built up a neat pile composed of alternate banknotes and blanks. The smell of the secret compound was preposterous — it conveyed memories of ancient battlefields in hot sunlight, questionable eggs, and the odour of the fish that goes into the Café Nouilles in wooden boxes, which makes even strong fish–porters unwell — and mingling with it came the ape–man's breath, charged with garlic and Brie cheese and twistgut brandy. It was not by any means a garden of roses. Still, I built up my tower of beautiful new notes and nice clean paper, and then wrapped it in strong vellum, which I carefully sealed.

" 'Watch,' I said, 'I now place the parcel in the press. I tighten the clips ... one, two, three, four. Good. Now I light this spirit–lamp, and very firmly close the lid. Now we wait.'

" 'How long?' 'Four hours. The temperature must be kept at about eighty–eight centigrade. After that it must be allowed to cool slowly for another four hours. Then we open the parcel, and your money is doubled.' Medved paced the room. 'It seems too good to be true,' he said, 'but if the worst comes to the worst, I shall have lost only eight or nine hours of time. Pedro, stand guard over that machine!' Pedro took from his bulging pocket an indescribably sinister revolver. Then we waited. Medved smoking cigars; Pedro picking his nails.

"Two hours passed. I fussed with the thermometer. Three hours passed. The atmosphere was tense. Four hours. 'Ten more seconds,' I said, looking at my watch — 'One ... two ... three ... four ... five ... six ... seven ... eight ... nine ... *ten* — open up!' and I tore off the lid and pulled out the bundle, steaming and hot. 'Blankets!' I shouted, 'Blankets!' Medved tore three thick blankets off his bed, and we wrapped the parcel in them and put it in front of the fire.

" 'Pedro, guard that parcel!' Pedro squatted over the parcel like a cannibal guarding a victim. Another hour passed. 'Is all this waiting essential?' 'Yes, it is. Let that bundle cool too quickly, and you'll get only half an impression, and the money will be spoiled, too. Besides, the paper must also dry slowly. You must have patience.' Medved helped himself to another cigar. An hour and a half more went by. I began to manifest signs of nervousness. I paced the room, biting my nails.

"Footsteps sounded in the passage. Pedro rose, and cocked his revolver. Medved went over to his bundle of money and prepared to defend it with his life. The footsteps passed. We all sighed with relief. I locked up my little machine and put it back in its case, together with all the little bottles. 'Another half-hour to go.' 'Thank God,' said Medved.

"And at that very moment, there was a thunderous knocking at the door — heavy truncheons; we all recognised the sound — and an unmistakable voice roared 'Open that door! In the name of the law!' I had hysterics. 'The money!' I said to Medved, in a terrible whisper. 'Hold it! Guard it! Don't open it! It will all be spoiled!' He clutched it to his bosom. Then I said: — 'My God, the machine!'

" 'Open that door or we break it down!' shouted the police. I seized the machine, and rushed out by the fire-escape. 'Guard the money with your life!' I shouted. Just then, the panels of the door began to crack. Ho–ho–ho–ho–ho–ho–ho–ho!"

Karmesin stopped for breath.

"Well?" I asked.

"Well! What do you think? When Medved opened his parcel, he found two thousand neat pieces of newspaper. I found a hundred thousand marks — very damp and malodorous, it is true, but very acceptable. It was the oldest trick in the world — switching similar parcels. Bah, fools!"

"But the police?"

"Police? They were three men whom I had employed to come in at that moment. But Medved did not realise that until he opened the parcel. Then he saw that he, Medved, the fox, had been taken in by an ancient swindle and a common Chinese–puzzle cabinet. He could do nothing, not even complain to the police. But it shows you how, by means of an atmosphere, you can get even blood out of a stone. It all goes to show the folly of human vanity."

Karmesin and the Tailor's Dummy

Karmesin nudged me, and said: — "Look at this."

I looked. A young man was walking towards us — a beautiful young man, dressed like an actor in a tight grey suit, a silk tie that made my mouth water, a hat that must have cost three guineas, and a magnificent pair of crocodile–skin shoes. As he passed, I caught a whiff of violet scented brilliantine.

"*Ekh!*" said Karmesin, "Barbarians! Is there any animal more absurd than man? No. Observe me that youth. Pfui! He encases himself in the wool of a sheep; knots about his neck the guts of a worm; has a reptile flayed to cover his feet; skins a rabbit to put on his head; and smears his hair with the fat of dead bullocks impregnated with the juices of squashed plants. Can you imagine an ape being so stupid as to want to cover itself in the skin of a debutante, and wear round its neck a string of beads composed of the teeth of a politician? Only among men is it considered a symbol of virtue, to hang oneself with such dead animal matter — silks, feathers, bits of stone! — *Tcha!* Yet for these things, nearly all crimes are committed. Only man is vain."

I could not refrain from saying: — "All the same, I watched you trying to take the shine off the seat of your trousers by scraping it with a razor–blade, the other day; and you raised blue murder when you cut the cloth."

Karmesin gave me a frightful look, and said: — "You had better be careful! Nature has placed an enemy in your mouth, to steal your brains away. If I attach some importance to dress, it is because I know that the world is full of fools who worship it. I use clothes: I am not their slave. Yet the desire for clothes, when it gets hold of a man, may be as destructive as drunkenness, drugs, or the woman–fever. I knew a man who used to starve himself in order to buy expensive neckties. Having bought one, he would put it on, and then stand in an elegant attitude outside the Café Anglais, ostentatiously picking his teeth. Indeed, one of my very earliest essays in crime was inspired by the clothes–fever of a bank–clerk."

"Were you very young then?"

"No, not very young. If I were writing a textbook of crime, a Guide to Easy Money, I should say, first of all: — *If you wish to become a successful criminal, never start too young. Lay your plans. See much of life and men. Observe human behaviour. Work alone. Choose, first of all, a fool–proof scheme; then start, coolly and cautiously, as one starts any other commercial enterprise.* Of course, I was an exception. I am a creative genius. I first conceive a crime–story, then make it come true. Besides, I started with one great advantage: I was a lawyer."

"Were you?"

"Yes, fully qualified, and even with something of a practice. If I were running a training–school for criminals, I should article all my pupils to solicitors. Nobody has less respect for the law than a solicitor. He has uncovered its nakedness: he has peeped under the sombre robes and observed the corsets, trusses, superfluities, hollownesses, and blemishes on the body of Justice. I was practising in Paris, and doing tolerably well. I was, as you may imagine, a very shrewd young man: clear–sighted, clear–headed, full of commonsense, subtle, quick to seize opportunities — a perfect young attorney.

"I was, also, extraordinarily well–dressed. Clothes never made any impression upon me, but I knew their effect upon the world in general.

"So then, as always, I spent a great deal on dress. I got my coats in London: the great Fisher made my waistcoats, which were the envy of all Paris. Schall, who was a greater hatter than Gibus, made hats for me; and old Mathurin created for me cravats which caused men to say: — 'They are not cravats: they are poems!' My moustache, moreover, was superlative: you see, now, only the ghost of what it used to be" — Karmesin stroked the thirteen–odd inches of dense white hair on his upper lip — "A moustache such as one turned in the street to admire. I used to perfume it with Fougère Royale. Aha, what a man I was then! The brain of a genius animating the body of a Hercules, turned out like D'Orsay! Needless to say, the upkeep of such a body was an expensive business."

"But you say you had a good practice?"

"Ye–es, yes, but not as good as all that. I never could live on a small scale. It was an expensive business, I say. Besides, dressing as I did, could I live on a top floor in Montmartre? Ask yourself. No. I had a flat in the Avenue Victor Hugo. To cut it short, I found myself somewhat in debt ...

"Well. It was my habit to eat at Hammerschlager's, which was a fashionable café. It was a species of Quaglino's: one ate, and then listened to a kind of band — a gypsy orchestra composed of five Montparnasse tziganes. I went there every night. I was an honoured guest. The maitre d'hotel called me by name, which is an honour. I always occupied the same corner table, from which point I studied humanity and watched the beau–monde absorbing food and wine. And I noticed one peculiar thing: at about nine o'clock every evening, when the café was at its busiest, a young man would come in.

"He was a tall, slender fellow, fairly well made, sallow–skinned and dark–haired, with a long, silky moustache and large black eyes. He was dressed with extraordinary care, in a good frock–coat and trousers, and a grey waistcoat with little red spots, like the back of a plaice. His hair was curled. He carried a thin ebony cane with an ivory knob. You could see that this youth spent many hours before his mirror; touching his face, playing with his moustache, brushing his eyebrows, and even rehearsing the expression of dignity and reserve which pulled down his eyelids and tightened his rather well–cut lips. He came into Hammershlager's every night at nine; walked into the middle of the restaurant, looked into every face, turned, and slowly walked out again.

"I began to wonder why he did this. Was he looking for somebody? No; I was convinced that he was not. He always looked *at* everybody; but without scrutiny. It occurred to me that he looked at people in order to see whether they were looking at him. He was, then, simply one of those foolish young men who dress and walk about the city in order to be seen. I spoke to the waiter: — 'Adolphe, does that young man ever dine here?' 'Very rarely, monsieur.' 'How rarely?' 'Well, perhaps once a month — yes, about the end of every month.' 'And what does he eat?' 'Oh, very little, monsieur; a sole, an omelette, and half a bottle of wine, perhaps; never more than that.'

"Then I realised that this young man was one of those pitiable impoverished dandies, who leave the office at six, dine at a cookshop for ten sous, dress, curl up their moustaches, and then walk up and down the boulevards, and in and out of fashionable cafés. (I once knew a man who did the same thing merely to display his whiskers, which were exactly like those of the Emperor Franz–Josef.)

"I waited. One night, the young man passed close to me. His glance fell on my waistcoat: his eyes lit up. Just as he was passing, I touched his sleeve. 'Excuse me,' I said, 'but aren't you Monsieur le Baron de la Tour d'Azyr?' He blushed with delight, and replied: — 'No monsieur; I am M. Frédéric de Cassis.' 'Oh, a million apologies,' I said; and so we got into conversation ..."

"Well?"

"Well," said Karmesin, "he was a bank–clerk. He was eaten up with the desire for the life of a gentleman — clothes, tiepins, and some credit in a decent restaurant or two. He wanted to cut a dash, walk the boulevards, smoke good cigars, and strut like a peacock. This was his ideal. This was his ambition and his great yearning. He craved new clothes as a drunkard craves absinthe. He plunged into his one good suit with the ecstatic joy of a man dying of thirst plunging into water. He came of a good, but impoverished family. To dress was, for him, more important than to eat.

"I drew him out. His little soft soul emerged from its shell like a winkle on the end of a pin. He calculated that, with the equivalent of a thousand pounds or so, he could leave the country and join some of his more elegant relations in America. He wanted to steal some money from the bank in which he worked, but he was afraid. He feared pursuit, disgrace, degradation; the soul–destroying barrage of the cross–examination; the horror of a prison sentence; the perpetual stigma of the criminal, and — worst of all — the ultimate short haircut, big boots, and ill–fitting prison clothes.

"I laughed.

"*Here*, I thought, *I sit in Hammerschlager's Restaurant quietly eating an entrecote, and Fate deals me this handful of aces!* I said to him: — 'My friend, you have the good fortune to be speaking to Karmesin, the greatest criminal attorney in Paris. You shall steal your thousand pounds from the bank. You shall go to America with it. You shall never be prosecuted.'

" 'But how is that possible?' he asked.

" 'My friend,' I said, 'come with me.' I took him to my flat, and dazzled him with its magnificence. I showed him my bedroom. I opened my wardrobe, and displayed seventeen coats, thirty-two pairs of trousers, and. forty waistcoats; cravats of every shape, size and colour; and enough linen to stock a shop. 'Have you faith in me?' I asked.

" 'Infinite faith!' he replied, fondling a black silk waistcoat as a devout man might fondle a rosary.

" 'Then come to me tomorrow,' I said.

"He came to see me on the following evening, at seven o'clock. I showed him an envelope. It contained a ticket to America. Then I said to him: — 'Go back to your bank. Steal eighty to a hundred thousand francs. Bring them here to me. Then you shall have twenty thousand, and your passage to America, and I guarantee that there will never be any prosecution.'

" 'But how can you guarantee that?" he asked.

"I replied: — 'You shall see. I guarantee it. That is enough. Do as I say, and you are safe.' I talked to him. He needed little persuasion — particularly when I suggested to him certain details of my little plan of campaign.

"Two days later, he slunk into my flat at six in the evening, with a fat bundle of notes: eighty thousand francs. 'Your ship sails tomorrow,' I said to him, 'Here is twenty thousand francs and the ticket. Go.'

"He began to tremble. 'They will telegraph New York and arrest me when I land!' I said: — 'They will not.' (This, you understand, was some years before wireless telegraphy was first used by the police.) He left, half dead with terror, and that was the last I saw of him.

"Then it was necessary for me to move quickly, because I had my side of the bargain to keep. I went to see young de Cassis' family: a shabby-genteel stepfather, and a brutal-looking old lady who was his mother. 'Frédéric is in trouble,' I said. 'Who cares?' said Madame de Cassis. 'I can get him out of trouble,' I said. 'All the better,' said she, 'but don't ask me to put my hand in my pocket, because I shan't.' 'No, my dear lady,' I said, 'simply permit me to act on your behalf and his. It will not cost you a penny.' 'Well, in that case,' she said, 'proceed.' 'Very good,' I said, and went and saw the president of the bank.

" 'Monsieur,' I said, 'I have been approached by the family of M. Frédéric de Cassis. He has committed an indiscretion ... He has robbed your bank of about eighty thousand francs.'

"The old gentleman jumped as if I had stuck a pin into his calf. 'What? What? Robbed the bank? Me? Us? Of eighty thousand? Eighty? Eh? Eh? *Saperlipote de saperlipopette de sacré bon Dieu de Dieu ...*'

"I calmed him. I spoke reasonably to him. Why pursue this absurd young man with his vengeance. He was already probably in New York, or even further. Who knew? Who would benefit, since he had almost certainly gambled the money away and then fled? ...

" 'But our eighty thousand francs?' he said.

"I said to him: — 'Monsieur. The family of de Cassis are of noble Norman stock. They are very, very poor; but their honour is as dear to them as life itself. I am empowered to act for them. They cannot repay the full eighty thousand francs. If they could they would but they have raised every farthing they have in the world. Altogether, they have raised exactly twenty thousand francs, which they will be glad to pay back to the bank in full settlement. Take it! It is, at least, twenty-five centimes in the franc: better than a loss of a hundred percent. Take it, and drop all ideas of prosecuting this misguided de Cassis! Or leave it, and lose everything.'

"He argued for three quarters of an hour on matters of ethics and principle. But I am a man of personality, force, and charm. I could have handled three such matters before breakfast. He took the twenty thousand in full settlement of the deficit. Hence, young de Cassis had twenty thousand francs and his freedom, the bank had twenty thousand francs, and I had forty thousand. It was a fair and gentlemanly division, *chort vozmi*, and everybody was happy."

Karmesin laughed again.

"It sounds very risky to me," said I.

Karmesin nodded. "A little. But what would you have? At the very worst, they could only have refused to accept twenty thousand. In that case I should have given them forty thousand, and had only twenty for myself. But I knew the President, and my reputation was formidable. I had confidence. I knew I should never fail."

"And what happened to Cassis?"

"I lost touch with him. I said to myself: — 'Here is a fool; his clothes wore him — he did not wear his clothes! Then, about thirty years later I saw his photograph in an American magazine. Under the picture was a success-story: he came to America quite penniless and in rags, and worked his way to the Presidency of a National Bank. He was wearing an ill-fitting black jacket, and striped trousers of atrocious cut."

"And what did you do with your part of the money?"

"Oh, I forget. I think I paid my tailor, and replenished my wardrobe," said Karmesin.

Karmesin and the Big Flea

A street photographer clicked his camera at us, and handed Karmesin a ticket. Karmesin simply said: — "Pfui!" and passed it to me. It was a slip of green paper, printed as follows: —

> **SNAPPO CANDID PHOTOS**
>
> 3 Film Shots have been made of
> *YOU*
> —by our cameraman.
> Post this ticket with P.O. value 1 /–,
> to SNAPPO, JOHN ROAD, E.I.
> For Three Lifelike Pictures.
>
> Name ....
> Address ....

"There is an opportunity for you," said Karmesin. "Procure nine or ten dummy cameras. Give them to nine or ten men, with your printed tickets. Have an accommodation address. A reasonable number of your tickets will come back with shillings. It will be quite a time before anybody complains. If anybody does, explain: — 'Pressure of business: millions of customers'. In three or four weeks, you have made some money. Then you can start a mail–order business. By the time you are forty you may retire. *Voila.* I have set you up in life. I have done more for you than many fathers do for their sons. Give me a cigarette. Well, what are you laughing at?"

"Why don't you try the scheme yourself?"

Karmesin ignored this question and went on, in an undertone: — "On second thoughts, have real cameras and real films. That relieves you of the necessity for accomplices. Always avoid accomplices. Don't develop your film: just keep it. Then, if the police come, you say in–dignantly: 'Look, here are the pictures. Give a man a chance to develop them!' In this manner you can last for two or three months. Never trust any man. Work alone. And speaking of photography; keep out of the range of cameras. They are dangerous."

"Why?"

"I once blackmailed a man by means of a camera."

I was silent. Karmesin's huge, plum-like eyeballs swiveled round as he looked at me. Under his moustache, his lips curved. He said: — "You disapprove. Good! Ha!" and he let out a laugh which sounded like the bursting of a boiler.

I said: "I hate blackmailers."

"The man I blackmailed was a very bad man," said Karmesin.

"How bad?"

"He was a blackmailer," said Karmesin.

"Oh," was all I could say.

"It was a good example of the manner in which little fleas bite big fleas. The man whom he proposed to blackmail was myself."

"Make it a little clearer," I said.

"Certainly. It is very simple. We were going to blackmail Captain Crapaud, of the French Police. He, in his turn, was blackmailing a certain Minister. The man with whom I was working was a certain villain named Cherubini, also of the French Police. He, not content with blackmailing Captain Crapaud, also wanted to blackmail me."

"On what grounds?"

"He was going to blackmail me, because I was blackmailing Captain Crapaud; and blackmail is a criminal offence, even in France. All he had to do was, obtain evidence that I was blackmailing Crapaud."

"All this is very complicated."

"Not at all. It is childishly simple," said Karmesin; and, having borrowed a cigarette, he proceeded to explain: —

Captain Crapaud (said Karmesin) was a man with whom it was impossible to feel sympathy. He was, if you will pardon the expression, a filthy pig. It is not usual to discover such men in high executive positions, in the police force of any great country, such as France. But as you know, such things happen. He had acquired a sort of hold upon a very great politician of the period. And he was using this man for all he was worth, which was plenty. This Crapaud was playing the devil. Like that other police officer, whose name, I think, was Mariani, he was using his office for purposes of personal profit. He organised burglaries, arranged the return of the loot, took rake-offs from this side and that; was responsible for many murders. He was a dangerous man to play with — a French equivalent of your own Jonathan Wild.

There is the basis of the situation: Captain Crapaud was holding a certain power, to the detriment of law and order; and his power was built upon a certain incriminating letter which he held.

You understand that? Good.

Now Crapaud had an underling, a species of stooge, a wicked little Corsican named Cherubini. This Cherubini was a bad man. He combined nearly all the vices, and, as is usual in such cases, was always short of money, although his income was far in excess of the normal. You know the type: his dependents starve, that he may bathe a couple of demi-mondaines in vintage champagne. *Pfui* on such wretches, I say! And *pfui*—and *pfui!* Tfoo! One spits at the very thought. Cherubini was little and rat-like. He had prominent front teeth, and no eyes worth mentioning. He would stop unhappy girls, and say "Be nice, or else …" But he had a weakness for the more elegant type of woman; and that kind of weakness costs money. Always beware, my friend, of the underling with luxurious tastes, for the time will come when he will nail you to the cross.

I met Cherubini in Cannes. He was going around like a Hungarian millionaire; with gardenias, and a gold-headed stick, and a diamond in his cravat, and an emerald like a walnut on his finger, and real Amber perfume on his moustache; smoking a Corona-Corona nearly as long as your arm … English clothes, English boots, silk shirts, polished nails — nothing was too good for this swine of a Cherubini.

I, needless to say, was a man of superlative elegance. I believe I have mentioned that my moustache was practically unrivalled in Europe. Yes, indeed, I am not exaggerating when I tell you that, while dressing, I used to keep my moustache out of the way by hanging it behind my ears. Nearly twenty-two inches, my friend, from tip to tip! However; it did not take me long to worm all the secrets out of the wretched little soul of this species of a Cherubini. He was second in command to the unspeakable Crapaud. Yes. That, in itself, was bad enough. But he was a traitor even to his master.

I will cut it short. Crapaud had a hold upon the Minister ... let us call him Monsieur Lamoureux. Follow this carefully. Crapaud also had a hold upon Cherubini. Do you get that? Good. The Minister Lamoureux wanted very much to break away from the clutches of Crapaud, and was prepared to pay heavy money for the letter which Crapaud held.

Was this letter procurable? No. But there was an alternative to procuring it, and that was, to incriminate Crapaud in such a manner that he would be glad to part with the letter incriminating the Minister.

But how could one incriminate Crapaud?

Cherubini had a plan.

There was one thing which, in France, could never be forgiven or forgotten; and that was Treason. Out of any other charge, it was possible for a man with influence to wriggle; but not Treason. There was a spy scare at the time. (It was a little before the infamous Dreyfus affair.) If one could prove that Crapaud was receiving money from German agents, in return for information, then one had him.

"But is he?" I asked.

"Yes," said Cherubini, "Crapaud is the outlet through which so many confidential matters concerning internal policy leak through to Germany. He receives, in his apartment, Von Eberhardt of the German Embassy; and receives, in exchange for certain information, a certain sum of money. If only one could prove this ..."

I asked: — "Have you means of getting into Crapaud's flat?"

"Yes."

"Then the whole matter is simple," I said. "Find out the exact moment when the money is likely to change hands, and take a photograph. A good photograph of Crapaud, taking money from Von Eberhardt, would be enough to hang him ten times over."

"Yes," said Cherubini.

"There is only one drawback," I said, "A camera is too cumbersome." This, you must remember, was before the days of the Candid Camera, and the lightning snapshot.

"Not at all," said Cherubini. "The police in Paris are beginning to use the portable camera invented by Professor Hohler. This camera can be concealed under an ordinary overcoat, and has a lens good enough to take a clear picture by strong gaslight."

"Can you get one?" I asked.

"Yes."

"Then what are you waiting for?"

"I am afraid," said Cherubini.

I paused; then asked: — "How much would there be in this?"

"How much? Why, two or three hundred thousand francs," said this rat of a man.

"Then have no fear. *I* will take the photograph, if you get me into Crapaud's flat at the right time."

Bon. It was agreed.

We arranged to go to Paris together, and settle the affair.

"I have entrée to the flat," said Cherubini, "and I know it like the palm of my hand. It is simple." And he added: — "But you must do the photography, mind."

All right. I will skip the tiresome details concerning the house, and so forth. It was a huge place in the Avenue Victor Hugo, with rooms as large as three rooms such as are built nowadays. The salon was something like a football field — vast, I tell you, and most luxuriously carpeted. The furniture in that room alone must have been worth four or five thousand pounds. Rare stuff. This pig–dog of a Crapaud did himself well. Near the window, there was a deep alcove, with another little window, or air–vent, at the back of it.

It was from this place that I was supposed to work. Cherubini had keys, and everything necessary. He also supplied me with the camera; a nice little piece of work, not dissimilar to the Leica or Contax camera of the present–day. I believe, in fact, that the Hohler Camera was the father of the candid camera. I was smuggled into the alcove, and there I waited for four hours, not daring to move. It was not very comfortable, my friend. However, in due course Crapaud arrived, with his friend Von Eberhardt. They sat. I was admirably in line with them. They conversed. I photographed them. They drank. Again I photographed them. They patted each other on the shoulder. Click! Again. Crapaud took out an enormous gold cigar–case, and offered Von Eberhardt a cigar. Again, click! Then, at last, the German took from his pocket a large roll of banknotes, and held it between his thumb and forefinger. Crapaud grinned and produced a sheet of paper. Then, as the paper and the money changed hands — click! Perfect.

Another hour passed before Von Eberhardt left. Then, as Crapaud went to escort his visitor to the door, I was up and out of the window, and away. You would never believe, looking at me now, how very agile I used to be. I thought I saw another figure slinking away in the shadows, but the night was too dark. I got to the street, and walked quietly home, where I developed my plates.

They were beautiful. The glaring gaslight, amply reflected in a dozen mirrors, was perfect. The photographs were as clear as figures seen by strong sunlight.

The next day, Cherubini came to see me. There was something in the manner of the wretch which disturbed me a little. He looked me up and down with an insolent grin, and said: —

"Captain Crapaud's apartment was broken into, last night."

"So?" I said.

"Watches, rings, trinkets, and money, to the value of fifty thousand francs were stolen," said Cherubini.

"Yes?"

"You were in the apartment, Monsieur," said Cherubini.

"Oh?"

"Yes. You see, Monsieur, *I* was behind *you*, also with a camera."

"Indeed?" I said.

"Indeed. And I am afraid that it will be my duty to have you arrested for the crime."

"Oh."

"Unless, of course, you are prepared to …"

"Pay you off, I suppose?" I said.

"Fifty thousand francs," said Cherubini.

"And otherwise?"

"Listen my friend," said Cherubini, throwing himself into a chair, "We are men of the world. I will put the cards on the table. The plates in your camera were duds, useless. You have no pictures. I, on the contrary, have some excellent ones of yourself in Captain Crapaud's flat."

"Any decent counsel could kick that case full of holes," I said.

"Oh no. Not by the time Crapaud and I have finished with it," said Cherubini. "Oh, my friend, my friend, you have no idea what evidence our boys would find, if once they searched your rooms."

"So I was caught, was I?" I asked.

"Like a fish in a net."

"But Von Eberhardt …"

Cherubini laughed. "Do you imagine that we would let you into the place with a camera? I mean, with a workable camera? With a camera loaded with proper plates? Be reasonable, Monsieur, be reasonable. There is nothing but your word, concerning Von Eberhardt. Who would believe you? No, no. You had better pay, my friend; you really had."

"And if I thought of all that, and took the precaution of changing the plates?" I asked.

"It would still have made no difference," said Cherubini, "The shutter of your camera would not work."

I rose, and seized him by the throat, slapped him in the face, and threw him to the floor.

"Listen," I said, "I would not trust you as far as I could see you. I saw through your game from the first. I had the shutter adjusted, the lens arranged, and the plates replaced. The camera was in perfect order. I will show you some pictures," I said; and showed him.

He was silent. Then I said: — "And now the ace of trumps. You remember how Crapaud offered Von Eberhardt a cigar?"

"Well?"

"Look," I said, and threw down a print. It was an excellent photo. One could see Eberhardt, Crapaud, and the unmistakable luxury of the salon. "Take that magnifying glass, and look at the cigar-case," I said. Cherubini took the large lens which I handed him, and looked; shrieked once, and looked at me.

Clearly defined in the polished lid of the case was an image of Cherubini, lurking behind the curtains, perfectly recognisable.

"Who wins?" I asked.

And Cherubini said: — "You win."

"And now who goes to Devil's Island?" I asked.

Cherubini simply said: — "How much for the plate?"

And I replied: — "Tell Crapaud this: — If he does not give me that letter of the Minister Lamoureux, then the day will come when one of his superior officers will hand him a revolver containing one cartridge."

"You are mad," said Cherubini. Nevertheless, three days later Crapaud's nerve broke, and I got the letter, which I returned to the Minister.

I asked Karmesin: — "What, you returned it free of charge?"

"Certainly," said Karmesin. "I simply asked him to pay my expenses."

"How much?"

"Chicken-feed. Fifty thousand francs," said Karmesin, "But am I a blackmailer? Bah."

"And Crapaud?"

"He left the country very suddenly, and, I believe, came to an evil end in the Belgian Congo, in the time of the Congo Atrocities. Probably some cannibal ate him. Or a lion. Who knows? Perhaps an elephant trod on him. I hope so. He was a villain. He was also a fool. He overreached himself. I was not the first person whom he had tried to blackmail in that manner. Only he was a little too clever. It should be a lesson to you: never be too clever. Also, beware of cameras. And furthermore, remember the folly of Crapaud, and if ever you come into possession of an incriminating document, you will know what to do."

"What?"

"Photograph it immediately," said Karmesin.

Karmesin and the Raving Lunatic

"Jewels? Haha!" said Karmesin, pushing his nose against the jeweler's window. "I know all about jewels. Look there. What for a diamond is that? Three hundred and twenty–five pounds for that yellow rubbish? Hoo! It is worth exactly one hundred and seventy–five. Only, people like big stones. Women particularly. They would rather have a miserable discoloured diamond as big as a hazel nut, than a small, perfect, white stone. I like diamonds. I have collected them."

"What, bought them?" I asked.

"Only a fool buys diamonds," said Karmesin, eyeing an emerald as a hungry boy looks at a pie. "The proper thing to do, is steal them. As a jewel thief, I was probably the greatest of all time ...

"Listen. Did you ever hear of the Betzendorfer affair? A diamond bracelet worth twenty thousand pounds, and an emerald valued at five thousand pounds, were spirited away."

"I seem to have read something about it, somewhere," I said.

"I did the spiriting," said Karmesin.

"It is one of those unsolved mysteries, isn't it?" I asked.

"Ptah!" said Karmesin. "There is no such thing as an unsolved mystery. Always, there is somebody, somewhere, who has a solution. What the police cannot put their great red hands on is an unsolved mystery, eh? *Pfui* and *pfui*, fifty thousand times *pfui* on such claptrap! Most people are dumbheads, my young friend."

"Come away from this window," I said.

"Bah. What is there in that window? Rubbish. Chicken food. Twenty thousand pounds would buy the whole shop. Am I to be interested in such small change? All right, let us walk on. Have you the price of a cup of tea?"

"I have threepence."

"I have threepence also."

I produced my money.

We sat in a teashop. "Tea!" said Karmesin to the waitress, with the air of a man calling for a magnum of *Pol Roger*.

"You were talking about a bracelet."

"The Betzendorfer affair? Aha. Listen ...

"It happened in Vienna," said Karmesin, "a number of years ago. I was living there. Vienna is a nice city. It was full of money. I was prosperous. Women turned to look at me in the street. Men gnashed their teeth when they saw me. What a figure of a man I was. A joy! A dream! But listen. I will tell you."

One day I was out walking, when I saw something which made me stop. It looked like a little firmament of stars, collected by a god, and imprisoned in a barred window.

It was the diamond bracelet. Ah, my young friend, what a diamond bracelet! Who could believe that crystallized carbon could contain so much pure light!

The bracelet was not priced, needless to say. One does not stick a ticket on the moon! But I calculated that it would be a good twenty thousand pounds worth of anybody's money. It came into my mind that Fate had sent me to Vienna simply to get that bracelet. I determined in that moment to steal it.

I went away and thought. When I think, something happens. I mean to say, I do not think in vain. I am, you understand, a man of genius.

In those days, Vienna was a home of psychiatry. Every lunatic in the world went to Vienna, either to start a new science, or to be cured of a non–existent state of mind. Psychiatry was the new fad. I do not deny that some people are psychiatric cases. Indeed, most people are. But not the ones who rush to psychiatrists to be cured. They need only to be cured of their desire to be cured.

There was Freud, of course. That man of genius was the master of them all. He did not toy with society cranks. No. He simply worked. But Freud was Freud. Next to him, the most fashionable psychiatrist was a certain Professor Trotz. Trotz was a clever fellow. He was, I believe, a good psychiatrist. But he liked luxury and money, and played the prevalent crazes for all they were worth. Society women flocked to his sanatorium, from every part of Europe and America. He had a huge house, full of impressive attendants.

As soon as I thought of him, I knew that the diamonds were mine. You see, he was well known, but not much photographed. Sometimes a picture of him would appear in a society magazine: He was a very big, impressive man, with a moustache like that of the Kaiser Wilhelm. It was very nice. I went to see him one morning, presenting the card of one of the noblest French families. "I am the Duc de Bourgogne," I said.

He purred like a pussy cat, for the Duc of Bourgogne was one of the wealthiest men in Europe.

"I wish to consult you," I said. "But this is a matter of the utmost delicacy. It concerns my unhappy brother."

"Yes?"

"In every way but one, my brother is sound," I said, "but he has one peculiar aberration."

"And what is that, Monsieur le Duc?"

"He has some fixation which distresses us very greatly."

"Tut tut."

"Any mention of jewels drives him mad."

"But exactly how, Monsieur le Duc?"

"If, for example, you showed him a diamond bracelet, he would become violent."

"But how interesting!"

"Indeed the very mention of the word 'jewel' drives him into a meaningless frenzy. At first, we thought that it would pass. But instead, it grows worse," I said. "Sometimes, he raves and shouts simply at the thought of jewels. It is very disconcerting."

"You have my sincerest sympathy," said Trotz.

"If you can cure him," I said, "you may name your own fee. I would pay anything in the world, to cure my dear brother."

"I shall be happy to help."

"But," I said, "you understand; he must not know that he is being brought to a psychiatric sanatorium."

"Certainly not."

"What I propose to do is, bring him here on some pretext, and leave him with you."

"A good idea. When do you propose to bring your brother?"

"Tomorrow," I said.

"Good. And at what time?"

"Shall we say four?"

"Perfect." He made a note.

"Now," I said, "I wish you to accept at least part of your fee in advance."

"I couldn't think of it."

"But I insist, Professor!"

"Ah, well, if you *insist*, Monsieur le Duc ..."

From a wallet as fat as a pig, I took then thousand *schillings*, and flicked them down. He thanked me.

"Pooh!" I replied. "And now be so good as to inform your servants that when I arrive tomorrow at four, they must show me to your waiting room without inquiry or hesitation."

"But certainly, most certainly, with the very greatest pleasure in the world, my honored Monsieur le Duc!"

Bon. It was all running as smoothly as oiled steel. My next step was to visit the jeweler. I asked for the proprietor of the shop, and presented a card. What card? Why, the card of Professor Trotz, of the Trotz Sanitorium!

"I am Professor Trotz," I said.

"Ah, yes," said the jeweler.

"I am about to become engaged."

"A thousand congratulations."

"But it is not yet officially announced. I wish to purchase a present for my fiancée. Something really fine. That bracelet, for instance ..."

He showed it to me. Ah, what a bracelet that was! It took all my self control to prevent myself from trembling. Its price was colossal. No matter. Nothing could be too good for my fiancée; for the bride of Professor Trotz; for the stupendously wealthy Madame Vanderkook, the widow of the fabulously wealthy Mynheer Vanderkook who owned most of the Dutch East Indies ...

"Naturally," said the jeweler, "one cannot give a small present to a lady like that; oh no."

"She is at present indisposed."

"Ah?"

"She is in fact a patient at my sanitorium."

"Ah ..." The damned jeweler had the insolence to wink at me. The psychiatrist had caught a wealthy client, he thought. I gave him a terrible look.

"I should want you, therefore," I said, "to come and show the bracelet to the lady herself, at the Trotz Sanitorium. You may come with me. Let her choose for herself. I shall also want an engagement ring, an emerald, not too dear. Something about five thousand pounds, six maybe ..."

Hah. It was as good as done. He put the bracelet and the ring into a leather case which he chained to his wrist, and showed me an automatic pistol in a holster under his jacket. "We must take no chances," he said.

We took a taxi, and arrived at the Sanatorium at four o'clock. The doorman let me in, touching his hat. The butler bowed, the nurses prostrated themselves to the ground. The burly attendants practically kissed my feet. There could have been no doubt in the mind of the jeweler that I was the Professor, the owner of the Sanatorium. I took him to the Professor's ante-room, and said: "Now, if you will please let me take the bracelet and ring in to my fiancée, and wait here, I shall be with you in one minute."

"Pleasure, Herr Professor Trotz, infinite pleasure!"

He unbuckled the bag and gave me the jewels. I walked into the Professor's room, and whispered: "Sssssh! Not a word. He's waiting out there. Let me out at the other door. I can't bear to be here when he finds out ..."

"I understand," said the Professor.

He let me out at the opposite door, and away I went, with the beautiful bracelet in my pocket.

Karmesin laughed until tea got into his bronchial tubes; after which he coughed, and beat the table with his huge fists until I slapped his back. Then subsiding, he said: "It was a joke. It was a scream. The Professor went out. The jeweler said: "Are the jewels satisfactory?"

"There, there," said the professor.

"But my diamonds?"

"Hush, hush, and let us talk it over."

"My diamond bracelet! My emerald!" screamed the jeweler, and pulled out his pistol. Trotz disarmed him with a kick on the wrist and called for the attendants, who, in ten seconds, had the unhappy man strapped in a strait-waistcoat.

Twelve hours passed before anyone realized that he was not a Duke's brother, but a swindled jeweler. And then it was much too late. I was on my way to Warsaw, disguised as an Indian Maharajah. I look very well in a turban.

It was good fun. It was a lovely bracelet. The emerald, also, was magnificent. I like emeralds. They bring me luck. They were jewels, I tell you.

But now, what do you get? Rubbish, nonsense, glass, valueless dirt! I would not take such diamonds as we were looking at, for a gift. No, not if you paid me, I wouldn't take them. Have you the price of five cigarettes? No? Bah. Let's walk ...

Karmesin and the Unbeliever

"Idiot!" said Karmesin, "only fools believe nothing. There are two kinds of ass. One believes all he hears. The other believes nothing. You belong to the latter species. I tell you things, and you simply listen, and afterwards laugh. I would bet that you believe less than fifty per cent of the things I have told you. Yet I pass as a truthful man."

"You *pass* as a truthful man," I said.

"Bah. I seem to remember your selling stories which I told you. You have cashed in on me. You live on me. I support you. In one of those ill-written and badly constructed pieces of literature, you referred to me as Either The Greatest Liar Or The Greatest Criminal The World Has Known. I disapprove of this."

"Um?"

"Yes. Yet if I told you that every word I said to you was true, what would you say?"

"I still wouldn't necessarily believe it."

"*Pfui!*" said Karmesin, and spat. Then he smiled. It was a smile of extraordinary softness. "But you are young," he sighed, "and therefore foolish. I knew an unbeliever like you, once."

"Yes?"

"Indeed. I met him on a cliff."

"What happened?"

"You will not believe me," said Karmesin.

"Oh, yes, yes."

"I would guarantee that you will not."

"Tell me, anyway."

"Then give me a cigarette," said Karmesin. He sat still, looking at me. It is difficult for me to express just how that steady, dark stare affected me. I felt that what he was about to say simply *must* be true. For the very first time in the years I had known him, Karmesin became desperately sad. "Listen," he said ...

I found myself a mass of nerves. I may say that any really important man must be a mass of nerves. Only when you become *aware* that your nerves predominate in your make-up, then, my young friend, is the time to give up work and relax. I went to Rocky Centre.

Why did I go there? Because it was quiet. It was damnably quiet. There was a population of about three thousand. Most of them lived by fishing. *Bon,* I like fishermen.

Bon. One night I walked out. It was a beautiful night; warm, calm, with a great round moon shining down. I sat on the verge of the cliff. A hundred feet down the sea licked at the rocks, and far out on the bosom of the Atlantic great patches of phosphorescence drifted and heaved.

Perhaps I dozed. It could not have been for more than five minutes. Then, when I awoke, I found that I had a companion. A man was sitting next to me: a man I did not like. He was small and thin, with a face — do you remember the rat, Medved? A face rather like that. I would not have trusted that man.

"I beg your pardon," he said. "But did I startle you?"

"Oh, no," I said.

"Lovely night," he said.

"Mm." I did not want to talk to the fellow.

"Look at the moon on the grass," he said. "It makes lights and shadows, eh?"

"Ghostly," I replied.

"Oh," he said. "Ghostly? Surely not? I don't believe in that kind of thing."

"Don't you?" I asked.

"No. Once you're dead, you're dead. Some people believe in an after-life. Not me. No such thing. I say: 'I want to *see* a thing before I believe it.' Don't you?"

I said: "I suppose so."

"If there were ghosts and things, where would we be? My goodness, we couldn't be sure of anything. For myself," he said, "I should hate to think of an after-life."

"Mm." I had to make conversation, so I said: "Live near here?"

"Yes," he replied, "I have that house over there."

"The Lodge?" I asked; and, sick or not sick, I became interested, because The Lodge was obviously the house of a wealthy man.

"Yes," he said.

I looked at him. He was dressed, but obviously not a gentleman. He had, indeed, something of the air of a valet — a gentleman's gentleman. He went on:

"You don't believe me, perhaps. Only right. I don't believe things I'm told. I'm an unbeliever. I only believe what I see. But the fact is, I do own The Lodge. I inherited it from old Mr. Thurston."

"Son?" I asked.

"No, valet. Kind of head cook and bottle-washer. I was everything to poor Mr. Thurston."

"Were you, indeed?"

"Yes. I pressed his clothes — not that he bothered about that, much, poor gentleman — and cooked his food.

"No shame in that," he went on. "There is a poem which says 'A civilized man cannot live without cooks.' I am a good cook. I think I can cook fish better than any man alive."

"Oh," I said.

"Yes!" He looked out over the sea, pointed down and said: "See those phosphorescent bits down there?"

"Well?"

"Poison."

"What?" I asked.

"That phosphorescent stuff. It's made up of animalculae. If you baled up a pint or so of that shiny stuff and drank it, you'd die. Of course, nobody'd go and *drink* it. But ..."

"Well?"

"Oysters can live on it. Mussels, too."

"Ah."

"Mr. Thurston liked mussels."

"Oh," I said.

"If," he said, "if a mussel ate that stuff, and you ate that mussel, do you know what would happen?"

"I can guess," I said. "One would die, I suppose?"

"Ah-ah," he replied. He looked at me again, and muttered: "Mr. Thurston liked mussels. He loved *Moules Marinieres*. I used to cook it for him. Of course, he was grateful."

"Yes?"

"He left everything to me," said the little man, looking up at me.

"Congratulations," I said.

"Thanks." He was silent for a moment, then, quite startlingly said: "Do you believe in ghosts?"

"No," I said. "Why?"

"Oh, nothing. Yes, I was telling you. I'm a gentleman now, you know. He left everything to me. At least, he really did. Only at the last moment, there came a long-lost nephew."

"Well?" I said.

"A long-lost nephew," said the little man, with a sneer, "a great stuck-up fellow, a cheapskate."

"So?"

"The old man was glad to see him: a fellow that wasted money like water, mark you. A profligate. The old man took to him more than to me; and I'd been with him for thirty years. He thought he was good-looking. So did old Mr. Thurston. 'My handsome nephew,' he used to say."

"Well, well, well."

"Yes. One evening they wanted to eat *Moules Marinieres*." I am very good at cooking *Moules Marinieres*."

"Well?"

He lit a cigarette, and said: "Nobody could prove anything."

"Prove what?"

"Well, they died — the old man *and* his nephew."

I gulped. Something about that horrid little man brought a bad taste into my mouth. It was obvious. He had discovered the poisonous properties of the phosphorescent animalculae and had poisoned the old man and his nephew. "So you boiled up a nice stew," I said.

"The secret of *Moules Marinieres* is frying with a bit of butter no bigger than a walnut, and some chopped parsley. *And the beards must be removed!* Not boiling. No. Well, they both happened to die. I didn't eat any, and I lived. And the original will held good, because he'd had no time to change it, and I was the heir. The house, the land, and two hundred thousand," said the valet.

"So you're a rich man," I said.

"Yes." He looked down, and shuddered. "Horrible rocks," he said, "horrible, horrible rocks. If you fell down on them they'd tear you to pieces like a dog's teeth."

"I can imagine it."

"It wouldn't hurt much, either."

I looked straight into his eyes. He had hideous little eyes which seemed to shine. "I think you're a murderer," I said.

"No," he replied. "No. Not a ... Well. Some people would be afraid of murder on account of ghosts and after–life and other such nonsense. But not me. When you're dead, you're dead. Eh?"

I said nothing.

He went on: "Well, I inherited. But it's lonely here."

"With murder on your conscience," I said.

He became angry. "What if I did? What if I did kill them? Who could prove it? And there's nothing to punish a man if the law can't prove it, is there?"

"I don't know," I said.

"But I do! There's nothing. When you're dead, you're dead. I can tell you that. I *believe* it!"

"So," I said.

He was silent. The moon shone down on him. The waves licked the rocks and over everything there was the hissing of the sea.

Suddenly he spoke again: "There's one thing I can't understand."

"Oh? What?"

"Just one thing. When you're dead, you're dead — I know that. But there's just one thing. You know ..." He stopped, and his face underwent a horrible change.

"Well, what?" I asked.

"You know everybody dies," he said.

"Certainly everybody dies," I said.

"But I can't! I can't die!"

I stared. He looked back, with a hell in his eyes, and said: "Look!"

And before I had time to step forward and stop him, *he walked right over the edge of the cliff!*

I am not a nervous man, but it was ten or fifteen seconds before I could bring myself to look down. I could see no sign of him: nothing but the rocks and the long swell of the sea.

Karmesin stopped. "What did you do then?" I asked.

"I went to town and yelled murder," he said. "I told them how a man had jumped over a cliff. They laughed at me. 'A little thin man in a black suit?' they asked. I agreed. 'Why,' they said, 'lots o' people see that. That's little Henry, old Mr. Thurston's valet, who died thirteen years ago come Michaelmas.'

"That's all," said Karmesin. "I suppose you won't believe this, too. I admit that I was sick, with nerves, and I also admit that I had been asleep for a few minutes. You will say that it was all a dream. But it was true. And the disbelief of fools never alters facts. Lend me a cigarette. I don't feel too good."

He finished his cigarette before I spoke to him again. "That," I said, "is quite a conventional ghost story. But I admit that I like the touch about the incredulity of the ghost itself. What happened after that? Did you go back?"

Karmesin looked at me. His large eyes rolled round. "What do you take me for?" he asked. "A fool?"

"It must have been frightening," I said.

He laughed. "I ought to have mentioned that I am practically devoid of fear. The next night I went back, and again the little man appeared. This time, I said to him, 'Sit down, my friend. Permit me to do some of the talking.' And so he sat down and waited.

" 'Now, listen,' I said to him. 'Unbelief is all very well, within its logical limits. *Bon*. You do not believe in ghosts. Good. Yet the fact remains that you are a ghost yourself, since you died a considerable time ago. Why try to fool yourself, my ghostly friend? Why try to fool me? Do you realize with whom you are dealing? I,' I said, 'am Karmesin. You must have heard of me. I have cleaned up more heavy capital out of scientifically—organized crime than any man in the history of the world. *Bon*. Then listen to my proposition ...' "

When the ghost realized who I was [continued Karmesin] I don't mind telling you that he was terrified of me. "Why?" I asked, "should you waste your time jumping over cliffs when you know perfectly well that you can't hurt yourself. Why be selfish? Why devote your nights to purely selfish suicidal attempts when you might be useful to your fellow—

men? I beg your pardon, to those who used to be your fellow–men? Let us get together." He was not insensible of the honor I was conferring on him — I, who rarely used accomplices. "Let us go into business together," I said.

We talked all night. In the morning I went to see Mr. Kildare, an estate–agent. The Lodge, a most beautiful old medieval house, was empty. I rented it, fully furnished, at a very low price. Then, making contact with a wealthy American who was living at that time in London, I offered to sublet The Lodge to them at a fantastically high rental, guaranteeing them a nightly manifestation of a hideous little ghost.

The American gentleman was delighted, but wanted to see the ghost before he signed the agreement. I invited him to The Lodge for a night, and let him see for himself. It worked beautifully. At six thirty in the evening he was horrified to see my little Henry glide across the room carrying a phantom pair of trousers. At eleven fifteen, when he was going to bed, he jumped a foot into the air as the icy little fingers of my Henry undid his bow tie for him.

"Okay, I'll take the place," he said. "What's your price?"

"Two thousand pounds for the summer."

"Two thousand pounds hell."

"Think how you can astonish your friends," I said.

"Right, I'll take it."

And he duly moved in.

Now, there were certain unpleasant aspects of Henry's character which I had failed to observe: he caused the cook to fly into hysterics by chucking her under the chin, and used to quarrel violently with the second footman below stairs. Again, no brandy was safe with Henry around, and on more than one occasion my tenant was annoyed to observe cigars floating through the air, obviously stolen from his cabinet.

But on the whole everybody was satisfied; especially when Henry grinned over the shoulder of the Duke of Tisket and Tasket as that progressive young nobleman was cleaning his teeth one Saturday night.

Yet things were not going quite as I had anticipated. I had meant to use Henry in a vast organization of hauntings. I meant to take several villas, castles, and granges, and to arrange for a genuine haunting once every night. A ghost can travel fast: time and space are as nothing to him. I was arranging to rent The Shambles, Dorking, for John J. Gilly, the automobile magnate, who was distinctly interested. But Henry had become unreliable. He spent all his time in The Lodge, scarcely moving out of doors. I reasoned with him: the constant lack of fresh air, I argued, must be very bad for his health ... But no.

I was puzzled, until the night of June 8th, when I was staying at The Lodge as the guest of my tenant. I could not sleep. I told you that my nerves were bad. At two in the morning I went downstairs to the library for a book. As I approached the door I heard voices: Henry's reedy little voice and that of a woman. I looked in. Imagine my surprise when I saw Henry, sitting on a sofa, making himself very comfortable with the master's brandy and cigars, with his arm about the waist of a lady in sixteenth–century dress, who was coyly holding her head underneath her left arm, sometimes lifting it up in order to whisper and giggle in his ear!

The miserable wretch had fallen madly in love with the spectre of Lady Jane Yule, who had been decapitated in the reign of Henry VIII, and who had been haunting The Lodge ever since! It was in vain that I pleaded with them, saying that respectable ghosts, like respectable servants, might quite easily haunt in couples, provided that they were properly married. But no. The Lady Jane would not hear of it. Go into service? She lifted her head up at arm's length in order to look down her nose at me.

My scheme had fallen through. I was not a loser by it, but my annoyance was very bitter indeed, my friend. Never hire accomplices, I warn you: they always let you down. I had to leave shortly afterwards to attend to the affair of the Cassidy Emeralds. And it was not until years later that I learned how my tenant had lured Henry and the Lady Jane to America with some absurd promise connected with a company directorship.

Inscrutable Providence

It was rough on my poor friend Karmesin. Finding a pound note in his possession for the first time in two months, he rushed out and bought a hundred cigarettes, and received a bad half-crown in the change.

"Look," he said, holding the coin in his fat, white fingers. He pressed: the half-crown bent. "Lead!" said Karmesin. "I could make better myself. Swindlers! Tramplers of the faces of the poor!"

"Take it back to the shop," I suggested.

"How am I to prove that it was the shopkeeper who gave it to me?" asked Karmesin. Then he laughed, and said: "Bah. It is all in the game. That shopkeeper would probably spit on the name of a pick-pocket, a forger, or an utterer of forged notes or coins.

"Yet let him receive a queer half-crown from a customer, and while that coin remains in his possession he is an enemy of society; his one desire is to pass it off on somebody else.

"Bah, I say! Let him keep it. He thinks he is smart, but God will punish him. I tell you, my friend, the great wrongdoer who knows good from evil stands a better chance of paradise than the smug citizen who slinks behind the skirts of the law to do petty misdeeds.

"I could keep this half-crown and pass it to some other unfortunate person. But how am I to know what misery I might cause by doing? No."

In spite of his fat and his age, Karmesin must have been as strong as an ox. He grunted, and tore the soft half-crown across, throwing the pieces out of the window.

"I heard a story," he said, "about a coin like that. Some men were playing cards. One of them lost everything, and borrowed a silver dollar for his fare home and his breakfast.

"On the way he was accosted by an unhappy girl in the last stages of despair. He was a good-hearted man; he gave her the silver dollar and told her to go in peace. Next morning she was found drowned; a bad dollar clutched in her hand. That bad dollar, you understand, had been the last straw.

"You see: the man of whom I told you; he was a good man, but Providence has used him for a tragic purpose."

Karmesin became silent. I said:

"Have you ever wanted to commit suicide?"

"No," said Karmesin. "Only murder."

"But I thought you disapproved of murder."

"I do, I do. Evildoers should be left in the hands of their destiny, which always destroys them in the end. Nevertheless, I was responsible for the planning of the Perfect Murder."

"How?"

"Come with me," said Karmesin, jingling the remains of his pound. "I have been your guest many times. Now you must be mine."

He took me to Xavier's Bar, and with an air of magnificence that sent the waiter skipping, ordered brandy.

"What is money?" said Karmesin. "Dross, rubbish. Thank God I have always spent mine as it came!"

He lumbered over to the Numbers Machine in the corner, inserted a shilling, pulled the handle down. The numbered discs whirred round and thudded to a stop — 3, 3, 3. Ten shillings dropped out of the machine with a jingle.

"Observe," said Karmesin. "There is one thing in the world which no man can resist; the jingle of cash. See — every eye in the bar is upon us. Now, come and drink your brandy, and I will tell you about my murder."

My scheme was not unconnected with a fruit-machine in a club not unlike this, not many years ago (said Karmesin). The victim was a man called Skobeleff, a man who richly deserved to die.

He was a criminal of the worst type, my friend; one who lives upon women. Skobeleff's specialty was blackmail. He had a genius for working his way into the affections of highly respected women.

You know how it sometimes happens, with the wives of great men. Their husbands, preoccupied with affairs, neglect them. They yearn for attention. It is only natural.

Then comes an intrigue, possibly an innocent intrigue — a friendship, quite often with an unworthy man versed in the wiles of the woman–hunter.

Skobeleff was such a man. Women found it difficult to resist him, for he had a handsome face, a fine imperial Guardsman's figure, magnificent blue eyes, the flaxen hair of an angel, perfect self-confidence, a boundless experience with women, and a voice more melodious than harp–strings ...

He struck up friendships with several nice ladies of uncertain age. This was his line; he would profess pure love and need for spiritual companionship; and then, by devious shifts, manage to get his victim to write a tender note — you know, my friend, "just to read when you are not here": it is an old trick.

And it always worked. It always has worked. I tell you, and always will: for women are fools in their affection, just like men.

Having his note, he would begin to bleed the victim. She was, you understand, always the wife of a very great man; somebody who could not afford a scandal of any kind, even if she were utterly innocent. He had a heart of ice, that Skobeleff, and bled them dry. It was a hideous business.

And when he wanted to have a quiet drink he always sat in the Maecenas Club near Piccadilly — an elegant drinking–den, with several fruit–machines in it, at which numerous idiots lost money enough to choke a hippopotamus.

Now it came to pass that I was approached one day, by a woman for whom I entertained the deepest affection. She was the wife of a very famous French politician.

I liked her very much in a quite platonic and brotherly way. Yes brotherly is the word for it, for she was twenty years younger than me, and I had bought her an ivory gum–ring with golden bells on it for her to cut her teeth on when she was a mere liver–coloured handful of babe in long clothes.

She approached me now and now told me a sad story. She was in terrible trouble. She had involved herself with Skobeleff, and had written him letters. Now, he demanded twenty thousand pounds sterling. Otherwise, he would place the letters in the hands of her husband's political opposition; ruin him, ruin her, ruin everything.

By selling some jewels she could raise ten thousand, but Skobeleff would not take ten thousand. He said: "Twenty or nothing. I can sell these letters for twenty thousand anyway ..."

Could I help? Could I lend her ten thousand pounds?

I said that I could do better than that, and get the letters for her.

I did so. It is a story of common burglary. I went to Skobeleff's apartment heavily disguised, with a large revolver, made him open his safe, took the entire contents of it, together with the letters my friend had written, and, having knocked Skobeleff unconscious with the barrel of the gun, quietly made my departure. That was easy ...

But when I came to examine the other papers I had taken, I was horrified. I, Karmesin, was disgusted! The man had made indexes and ledgers of dirty crime. He had a whole career of vile blackmail laid out.

God knows what a trail of misery he was planning to leave in his wake. I only knew one thing; by stealing his papers, I had held him up only for a little while. Sooner or later he was certain to operate again.

The law could not touch him. If he left the country, he would operate elsewhere. I decided to take the law into my own hands. I approached him with a proposition.

I told him who I was, and he was impressed; he knew of the things I had done. Then I said to him:

"Do you know who lives in the flat above the Maecenas Club?"

"Old Lord Westerby."

"Do you know what he keeps in his safe?" I asked.

"No, what?"

"The Westerby Collar."

"The Westerby Collar!" said Skobeleff. "A hundred and eighty priceless emeralds, and the Green Devil Emerald in the centre!"

"You could help me to get them. I have an immediate market. We can get at least two hundred thousand. Help me, and I'll split with you fifty–fifty."

"But how?"

"Now listen," I said, "I will do the work. I will get the emeralds. What I am going to suggest is this: I slip upstairs and get the jewels. A diversion is created that draws everybody in the club into the fruit-machine room.

"You slip out on to the balcony in the room behind. That balcony stands directly underneath the servant's bedroom in the Westerby flat. We synchronise our watches.

"At midnight precisely, you step on to the balcony and I drop the jewels down into your hands. Then you rejoin the crowd in the next room, and nobody will ever know that you have not been there all the time. Next morning you meet me and give me the jewels ..."

Even as I spoke to him I could see the idea of a double-cross entering his treacherous mind. I could see it in his eyes.

"But how will you get everybody into the fruit-machine room?" he asked.

"At ten minutes to twelve," I said, "a man will win the jackpot on every machine in the place."

"If you can arrange that," he said, "you must be a wizard."

"I am a wizard," I said.

When I left him I looked up a man called Martin, a good little rogue who had had occasion to be thankful to me many a time, especially once when I supported his wife and three children while he spent a year in jail.

He was something of a genius of engineering; I mean, very clever with wheels and springs. Would he help me? He would have gone through hell and high water for me. I promised him fifty pounds.

His act was simple. At about eleven o'clock he had to come to the club with a bag, showing the official card of the firm that manufactured the fruit-machines. Then he was to unlock each machine, and adjust it so that the next revolution of the wheels would bring the total to Three Bars, which wins a jackpot.

That is a very simple matter for a man who knows how to handle his machinery. Normally, of course, your fruit-machine engineer sends the wheels flying round six or seven times before leaving the thing, just to see that all is well. But Martin would not do this, of course; and nobody would notice.

I told you: nothing attracts people like the jingle of money. There must have been a dozen machines in the club. The crash of a dozen jackpots would bring every member running from the next room; the floor would be knee-deep in silver. Everybody would be pulling handles, or stooping for fallen coins.

Then Skobeleff would come out on the balcony. He thought he ran no risk, for the secretary and commissionaire whom one had to pass before entering or leaving the club could both swear that he had been in there all the time.

Only I was not going to be on the next floor with a priceless emerald collar. I was to be at the darkened window of the flat across the road. In my hands there was to be a rifle. I was a perfect shot, and still am.

From that distance I could not miss. I should put a bullet in the centre of Skobeleff's forehead and wipe his evil presence from the face of the earth.

Martin was waiting in the street with a car. At ten seconds before twelve, as the theatre crowds filled the streets, he would jam the traffic; there would be a chaos of horns. He would make his engine backfire furiously. The sound of my shot would be unheard. It was perfect. And so it turned out.

A young fool called Poppins put a shilling in the fruit-machine and let out a deluge of coins. Others followed suit. The proprietor of the place came running, white in the face. The machines had gone mad! They were paying out jackpots!

The whole club poured into the room, eager to put a shilling in, or to see money coming out. Simultaneously, a fearful uproar broke out in the street below. Cars jammed in a black mass, honking like fury.

Martin's big black automobile banged and thundered, giving out clouds of smoke.

I got Skobeleff's head in line, took a careful aim. He was outlined against the light. I could not miss — I who have knocked the head off a running antelope at five hundred yards. I pressed the trigger.

Skobeleff shrugged his shoulders and walked back into the club. Remembering everything, planning everything, organizing everything so perfectly, I had forgotten to load my rifle.

Karmesin laughed. "Yet he deserved to die," he said.

"Well?" I asked. "Well? What?"

"Yes," said Karmesin. "It proves my point. Such men are always punished in the end. Nemesis is always upon them. They are never more than one jump ahead of a terrible vengeance. It is not for man to kill: only for God."

"But *Skobeleff?*"

"Skobeleff," said Karmesin. "He stayed in the club until one o'clock in the morning, then went home. Do you remember the big fire in the hosier's shop in Dublin Street, Piccadilly? Skobeleff lived above. He perished there that night.

"You see, in leaving that blank spot of forgetfulness in my brain, Fate was preserving Skobeleff for something terrible. A man cannot run away from his destiny."

"But how did you get into the flat exactly opposite the club, when you meant to kill Skobeleff?"

"Ha!" said Karmesin. "I got into it the same way as I got into it before: with a duplicate key. And I knew that the occupant would be on the balcony opposite. *It was Skobeleff's flat!*"

"And the fire?"

"Inscrutable Providence," said Karmesin. "When I found that I had forgotten my cartridges, I took my cigar out of my mouth and casually flipped it over my shoulder. 'Let Providence proceed with the matter,' I said.

"It was a ten–to–one chance against the cigar–end causing a fire. Well, it caused a fire, but not until Skobeleff was asleep. Providence! Fate! Skobeleff perished.

"It is right and proper that rubbish should be incinerated. So perish all rubbish. Another brandy?"

Karmesin and the Invisible Millionaire

"You are a damned fool, because you believe nothing," said Karmesin. "And yet, if I may coin a phrase, there are more things in heaven and earth than are dreamt of in our philosophy. Yes, indeed, if you will permit me to lapse into verse: things aren't always what they seem. When I told you about the affair at Rocky Centre you seemed not to believe me. Little Henry, the ghost of Mr. Thurston's valet, was something you could not swallow, yes? Yet he existed. Oh, yes! And twice! Oh, yes! I mentioned to you that, though I had a lucrative offer to make him, he went with an American millionaire to the United States, lured there on the premise of a company directorship."

"Bah," I said. "What would a ghost want with money, since he can't spend it?"

"Why, you confounded idiot," said Karmesin. "Don't you realize that a ghost, in order to have social status in the Shades, must have a treasury to gloat over? Haven't you read your books? Ghosts are as delicate about such matters as men and women: they need money in order to keep up their appearances. For example, one of the most respected phantoms in the spirit world is that of Atilla, the Scourge of God, whose fabulous treasure is still undiscovered, and who can, therefore, still boast about it. You mark my words, there was more than the merest superstition in the preoccupation of the ancients with the treasure that was buried in their graves. In Limbo, as elsewhere, you need a little cash in your pocket: for the spirits are but the shades of human beings, and are therefore still influenced by human follies. Have you never heard of a revengeful ghost? Yes. Very well then. Should a greedy or acquisitive ghost be so strange, therefore? I would not harp on my partnership with the ghost of Henry, if a certain topical indication had not arisen."

Karmesin pointed to a cutting from a newspaper:

Mystery Disappearance of Sago King
Ira K. Kiljoy Still Missing

F.B.I. Question Maxie Waxiendinero
We Say "So What?"

"Missing," said Karmesin. "Disappearance. *Pfui* and *pfui* and *pfui!* That means to say he went to his country club without notifying his relations; or visited one of his love-nests. The Bureau of Missing Persons will find him. To be lost in a country like the United States is like being a needle in a haystack: it is hard to find one, but one is there and may certainly be found. Now I don't know whether you ever heard of Dickson M. Sackbut, the Copper Baron. It was one of the most baffling mysteries of the century," said Karmesin, "and I only know the secret behind it."

He fumbled in a pocket and found nothing; said, peremptorily: "Cigarette!" He lit it, and went on. "Now listen."

Then he told the following story:

You will not have heard of Dickson M. Sackbut. I forgot: the maternal milk is hardly dry on your lips. You are a child. This happened in 1906, in America. Sackbut was a copper king: he had come from nowhere, and, by dint of doing nothing, had made a huge fortune. He was a decent kind of man, but a fool, who did not understand finance. If there was too much copper in the market, he simply flashed his ten-thousand-pound cuff-links and bellowed: "Then we must mine more and more!" In effect, he made a bit of a beast of himself, like all men who acquire great fortunes and don't know how to handle them. He could not think in terms of tens or hundreds: I liked him for that. He liked thousand, millions, billions. If he bought a girl a bouquet it turned out to be a van-load of gardenias; and though his early drinking had been black tea out of a dirty billy, in his latter life he was grossly insulted if his champagne was served in anything but a silver goblet. A mining-man, my friend; a wild fellow.

Bon. When I arrived in America in 1906, I met him in Chicago, and liked the man. He was very nice. There was something about him that appealed to my Russian sense of proportion — it was delightful to see him bathing barmaids in brandy, and beating the waiters. I saw him knock out Pig Iron Moloney with one left hook, for spitting on his newly-polished boots; and then smash up the Millionaires' Bar because his Sole Meuniere was not done to his liking.

Sta bene! He liked ladies. All right, all good men do. I like ladies, *chort vozmi!* He was fooling with a certain woman named Mrs. Twinkletoe — an absurdly pure woman, my friend, such as these ignorant miners love: a spinsterish matron with prominent teeth and bony shoulders; a thinker of beautiful thoughts. Rough men seem to like these caricatures of womanhood; or, at least, sentimental men who lead rough lives. She, however, was married to a certain Roger Twinkletoe of Schenectady, a kind of adventurer. Though they had been man and wife for years, one felt that there was nothing between them, if you know what I mean. You could not imagine making love to this woman, amiable though she was. The bones of her shoulders would have lacerated your enfolding arm; and she had hips like a giraffe. What Sackbut saw in her, God knows. He pursued her.

It happened that they were riding together in an open carriage when the horse shied, and she was thrown into his arms. A million people saw. Mr. Twinkletoe spoke of taking his father's sword from the wall and confronting the home-wrecker with cold steel. Father's sword, bah and *pfui* and *ptoo!* His father never had a sword and anyway, he never had a father. It ended with divorce proceedings, which Sackbut, in the state of his business, could not afford. You know what the American women are: one hint of home-wrecking, and they will start a landslide: though they always love a rake.

Sackbut had nerves. He wanted to negotiate, but dreaded the service of the papers. Yet he could not get out of Chicago. He was ringed around. He was a man whom any kind of incarceration would have driven mad — a man of the open spaces, if you get what I mean, whom fifty minutes in an opera-house afflicted with claustrophobia. And he dared not move out of his hotel-room! It was dreadful.

I had gone to Detroit on certain dirty business. A day after my arrival I received a wire as follows:

COME AT ONCE DAMN IT STOP KEPT BLASTED PRISONERS IN DAM BEDROOM BY DINGBUSTED PROCESS HYPHEN SERVER STOP HELP ME OUT BY

THE JUMPING JIMINIES OR COMMIT SUICIDE STOP SACKBUT HOTEL CROESUS CHICAGO

I received the wire at midnight, and wondered what to do about it. I was aware of the circumstances, and felt baffled. And so I sat and thought; and even as I sat and thought, I heard a nasty, shy little voice say: "Ahem! Mr. Karmesin?"

I looked, and saw nobody. Nerves? I said, in as calm a voice as I could: "Well?"

The voice replied: "Ah, still as brave as ever, I see," and, looking in the direction of it, I saw a mist appear, like breath on a mirror, just by the bathroom door. Then, out of this mist, my little ghost Henry appeared. He looked fatter; more prosperous.

"What the devil!" I said, "I thought you were in New York." "Honeymoon–trip." "Where's your wife?" The conversation was exceedingly staccato like that.

"Here," he said. "Oh, Janey!" And beside him materialised the spirit of Lady Jane Yule, coyly holding out her head between her hands to kiss me on the cheek.

"Drink?" I said. He replied that he had given up drinking. "Cigar?" No. I was astonished, for he had always been partial to a good Havana cigar. Then he said:

"I am in training. If you'll permit me to say so — you know how it is. We ghosts get around a little. Only the other day, I was saying to William Shakespeare — one of the Stratford–on–Avon Shakespeares, you'll remember, sir —" (I gestured impatiently.) "Oh, I'm sorry, sir. I didn't mean to take liberties. I was saying to Mr. Shakespeare — a nice man, sir, but no gentleman: he wouldn't have done for his Grace, sir — that although he was quite well known as a journalist, he would have done better if he could have got around a little. The people we ghosts meet!"

"That *nice*, Mr. Casanova!" said Lady Jane, coyly playing ball with her head.

"Yes. But one meets *useful* people too, Mr. Karmesin. Example? A couple of Biblical prophets, sir, who put me on to the winner of the Kentucky Derby; and, above all, Mr. Samson Trismagistus, a sorcerer. A man who knows all sorts of things. He was burnt alive in 1446. He had the gift of invisibility."

I started. "The what? Now look," I said. "Be a good ghost, Henry, and give one of your oldest and most intelligent friends the inside dope."

"Most intelligent? Ha! Do you realise that I have, by dint of enterprise, humility, and energy, succeeded in making friends with the sorcerers and magicians of all history? Oldest? I know Methusaleh personally. Come, come. But look here. I like you, Mr. Karmesin, and am prepared to make a deal with you; for a ghost, as you understand, must have a corporeal agent." He gave me a sort of Cheshire–cat smile, ingratiating.

"Ten per cent, of all monetary proceeds," I said quickly.

We compromised at twenty–five per cent, and I telephoned Sackbut. "How much is it worth to you?" I asked. "Don't be too stingy," I warned him.

"I'll give you the Sackbut Mine and fifty thousand dollars cash."

"Keep the mine and make it fifty–five thousand," I said. "Done? Then do exactly as I say. Don't forget. *Exactly* as I say. Always."

So I went with Henry and his wife to Chicago. It was then that we assisted in the greatest mystery of all time. What was it? It was this.

Sackbut, the millionaire, guarded on every side by process–servers, went into his bathroom to bathe, and locked the door. Water pouring to the floor below indicated that the tap was running. Suicide was suspected. They broke open the bathroom door. His clothes were in the bedroom, his bath–robe in the bathroom, together with his slippers but he was nowhere to be seen. There was no cupboard for him to hide in and no chimney for him to creep up. More mysterious still, the bathroom was locked on the inside, and the window, which was small, was twenty stories from the ground, with less foot–purchase than a fly could have taken advantage of.

He had disappeared into the novelist's thin air. It was Henry's doing, at my instigation, on the formula of the mysterious Trismagistus. The divorce proceedings fell through, for lack of material co–respondent.

Days passed. It was all very simple, of course. The millionaire was there, but invisible. We met him in the lounge of the hotel and discussed matters. I asked for my fifty thousand dollars. He said: "Bah!" I said: "Then stay invisible." He laughed in my face. "I'd like to stay invisible," he said, with a dirty laugh. "You'd be surprised at the things I see, and the way I get around. I was in Birdlime's office this afternoon, and caught him selling out Oleaginous Oil. It's good. I have my fun."

Then a nasty little voice by my side said: "Oh, all right. He won't pay. Very well, I'll make him visible again." The invisible millionaire laughed. "Allez–oop!" said Henry. And the whole hotel gasped. There at my table, naked as the day he was born, sat the millionaire. "Now," said Henry, while the millionaire struggled with the tablecloth and tried to cover himself. "As an invisible man, you have no civic rights. If I make you visible now, you'll be arrested, probably thrown into an asylum. Pay, therefore, Mr. Sackbut, without further delay. Yes?"

"Yes, yes. Only make me invisible again."

I caught his arm. Henry said another strange word, and the millionaire faded and vanished, just as the waiter came running up.

"There was a naked man at your table," he said.

"Pardon me!" I said, with a look such as only I can give.

He went away. "Now," said Henry, "lead us to the money."

We followed him upstairs to his suite without accident — except once, when the invisible Sackbut brushed against the Countess of Gaga on the staircase. He opened his door, lifted his mattress, and produced a great wad of money.

"There," he said. "Now make me visible again."

"Allez–oop!" said Henry, and there stood Sackbut before us.

"Damn you," said the millionaire, and went into the bathroom.

I reached a hand out for the money. It grew misty, wavered, and was gone. "Henry! Would you double–cross a friend?" I cried. His only answer was a wicked laugh. The money was gone. When the people of the hotel came up and found Mr. Sackbut in his bath they were thunderstruck, but he said:

"What the hell? I've been here all the time."

That was one of the very few occasions when I was swindled, and even then it was by no human agency.

Karmesin looked solemn. I stared at him. "And am I supposed to believe that?"

"Since it is true, why not?" he answered with an indifferent frown.

I could find no words to say, except: "And Henry? Did you see him again?"

"Many times, and I had my revenge too. But that is another story, as the poet said," said Karmesin, taking another of my cigarettes.

Karmesin and the Gorgeous Robes

Karmesin was cleaning his shoes, and you may take it from me that it was a sight worth watching. He took a bit of rag, and smeared the leather with polish, rubbing it in with all his force. Then he found a piece of linen, upon which he spat with a curious delicacy — *Tfoo!* — and proceeded to make the room shake with powerful twists and oscillations of his gargantuan body. His eyebrows jerked and his moustachios beat in the air.

"These shoes have lasted seven years," said Karmesin, gloomily. "They cost me seven pounds. I once pawned them for seven shillings. There is something mysterious about the number 7. I am reminded of the affair in the cathedral town ... *Tfoo!* The way to get a real shine on a shoe is, spit and polish. Hai, hai, when shall I again have seven–pound shoes on my unhappy feet?"

"Why does seven remind you of the affair in the cathedral town?"

"Seven. Seven. Ah ..." Karmesin sighed. "Do you remember the fairy–tale of Benaiah, Solomon's captain, who captured Asmodeus, the Demon King? They were passing a cobbler's door, outside which a man was ordering a pair of sandals strong enough to last for seven years. 'Ho–ho!' roared Asmodeus. 'What's this joke?' asked Benaiah. 'Why, that fool orders a pair of sandals to last seven years, when he is destined to die this very night ...' Seven is a strange number."

"But the affair in the cathedral town? Can I please have the story?"

"Now listen to me, my young friend," said Karmesin. "You insist on writing down every word I say to you. Only God and I know what a fearful mess you have made of the epic tales of crime I have been benevolent enough to tell you. How do you delude your Editor into publishing them? Do you pay him? Or is he a relation of yours? Heaven forbid: I would not wish my worst enemy to have a relation such as you. Number 7. There are seven days in a week, seven branches to the sacred candlesticks, seven heavens, seven muses, seven deadly sins, seven —"

"I have heard all this before ... Seven Pillars of Wisdom, Seven Ages of Man, Seven Year Itch — I know, I know. But the cathedral town!"

"The number 7 brings it very vividly into my mind. So, also, do these shoes. Seven-pound shoes are human vanity, my friend, and my cathedral story is not unconnected with that, also. Oddly enough, I was thirty-four years old at the time, and four plus three is also seven. Do you, my young friend, ever consider how mathematics —"

"You might as well cut out the arithmetic," I said.

"Only fools ignore arithmetic." Karmesin scrawled a number on a bit of paper, which he held concealed in his vast fist. "Quickly name me a number between five and twelve."

"Seven," I said. And immediately cursed myself for falling into the open trap.

Karmesin opened his fist and showed me the paper. The figure 7 was written upon it.

"Ninety-nine people out of every hundred will say that: try it some time. But what was I saying? Seven, seven, seven ... The cathedral town; oh, yes. A good story."

And, still polishing his shoes, Karmesin went on to his yarn. Here it is: —

Rouen — it is a pleasant town. Guy de Maupassant liked it, too. There is something vast and powerful about it. It would be all right if it were not for some of the people. The northern Frenchman is a hard-boiled fellow; genial, but full of tricks. Do you know the Norman legend of St. Michael and the Devil? No romance there, my friend: the Norman says that St. Michael filled the Devil up with heavy food and cider before beating him up. That is the Norman idea of smart business.

But I was speaking of number 7. I arrived in Rouen on the seventh of August, 1907 — my birthday. Most great men are born round about then: Napoleon, Longfellow, de Maupassant himself, Daniel O'Connell ...

So. You will ask why I went to Rouen. I will tell you. I went there for one definite purpose: to rob the safe of a horrible antique-dealer named Potdevin. He was a holy terror, that Potdevin, and the number of his shop was seven. He was a big, fat man — a kind of Antoine — a typical Norman, with carroty hair, a fierce face, and a cold blue eye

Karmesin and the Gorgeous Robes

devoid of pity. He was a glutton. It was said that he once ate a whole sheep, for a bet. And as for drinking, my friend, it was colossal.

That Potdevin was extremely rich and extremely unpopular. He was a moneylender, as well as a dealer in antiquities, and had a tendency to coerce his servant–girls to be very nice to him, just like a theatrical agent. "Be nice or else ..." His cunning was abysmal. His capital was derived from certain disgusting investments. It was Potdevin who had interests in twelve houses of ill–repute in North Africa and South France. He helped in the organization of certain shipping–orders ... human flesh, my friend. I heard of him, first, through a pitiful young woman in Ostende. She had worked her way back from God knows what in–famous part of Asia, and was preparing to go after him with a sharp pair of scissors. Women never kill with "blunt instruments."

I flatter myself (said Karmesin, gravely) that I have sometimes acted as an instrument of a just Providence. I reasoned with the girl. "Don't go," I said. "Leave Potdevin in my hands, and I will punish him. When I have finished with him, my child, then, perhaps, you may say your little say. Don't use scissors, but try a knife. Always keep your thumb firmly on the blade, and strike upwards under the ribs. A shotgun is best, but cumbersome to carry. If I were you," added I, "I should abandon the idea. But if, on the other hand, I were determined to carry it out, then I should get a shotgun and load it with buckshot. Then, walking with an ingenuous air into his shop, I would say, 'Would you care to purchase this rare gun?' and, pointing it at his unsuspecting stomach, let him have both barrels ..." But this is beside the point.

I wanted to punish Potdevin in a manner calculated to hurt him most. Shotguns, though messy, are almost painless. But the pocket of a miser, my friend, is a terribly sensitive spot to strike. I learned that he kept a great stock of antique jewels in his safe, together with a fabulous sum in gold and bonds; for he transacted much strange cash business, and, in any case, didn't trust the banks. Like all misers, he had to have great sums of money about him, just because he loved it so much.

So. I sent a colleague of mine to observe the layout of things. He returned with a report. The shop of Potdevin was crammed with innumerable rich objects, notable among which was a certain set of very rare robes. They had belonged to some Malay potentate of a bygone age, and were magnificent indeed. There was a pair of baggy trousers of the purest silk; a coat of gold, and a cloak of incomparable splendour. The work of fifty women, for a dozen years, must have gone into the embroidering of that stupendous waterfall of jeweled silk. Dotted with pearls, diamonds, rubies and emeralds, it was a dream, my friend. To complete the outfit, there was a very wicked sword with a wavy blade and an ivory hilt, and a steel helmet with a yellow plume. It was superb.

As soon as I heard about Potdevin's shop at Number 7, Rue Lebrun, I saw that everything would be easy. I could rob this wicked fellow, and punish him at the same time. I wanted his money, you understand; but I also felt that vengeance should overtake him ... And somehow, at the back of my mind, there hung the awfully sordid picture of the girl from Ostende — broken, you understand; sold into slavery, and creeping back a wreck beyond hope, with nothing left to live for but her bitter hate.

So I went with my friend — a reliable fellow of a bull-like strength — to see Potdevin at Number 7, on the seventh of August, in the year 1907. We looked over his stock, and then, seeing the robes, expressed ourselves fascinated, and asked the cost.

"Forty thousand francs," said Potdevin, without trying to boost his wares.

"What?" I demanded, with little more than rhetorical impatience.

"Not a centime less ..." The old devil seemed determined.

The haggling went on. I am a good bargainer, but Potdevin was a rock. Bit by bit we crept down, and at 35,000 he stopped dead and refused to argue further. I had conveyed to him, you see, by my manner, that I had set my heart on those robes; and he thought he was reading my soul, the poor fool.

"You are a devil," I said. "And a Norman devil at that!"

"Ah," he grunted, and laughed jovially. They are the very devil, these Normans!

"I will give you five thousand francs deposit now," I said, "and return with the rest tomorrow. Remember, this deposit secures the robes."

"But of course." He took the five thousand francs I gave him, carefully inspecting every note. Then he asked my name. "Hippolyte Leclerc," I replied.

"What, the great Leclerc? The actor? Really! I have often wanted to see you perform, but I am such a poor man, Monsieur Leclerc, and I can't afford the price. When you act, it is impossible to get in. And in any case, it would mean going to Paris."

"I will give you a couple of tickets tomorrow," I said. "You will see me wearing these superb robes of yours when I play *Tamurlane*."

"I should be very happy ... Theatres are so expensive ..."

We parted with every expression of goodwill. I knew I could rely on his keeping silent about the matter, for he was a much-hated man with few friends. And so, next day, at about three in the afternoon, we called again at Potdevin's shop.

"Have you the robes?" I asked.

"Yes. Have you the money?"

"Here," I said, taking out a packet of notes. Then I examined the robes again and said: "Monsieur Potdevin, would you do me a favour? We are roughly of the same size. Would you dress yourself in these robes so that I might see how I should look."

Potdevin laughed, with his horrid geniality. "But, of course!" It was not every day that he picked up twenty thousand francs profit on a set of garments, my friend! He shut the shop door, and, taking off his coat and shoes, pulled on the tasseled slippers, the shimmering trousers, and the high-buttoned gold coat. He buckled on the beautiful belt, girded with its wicked sword; placed the steel helmet on his carroty head, and slung that gorgeous cloak over his fat shoulders.

"There," he said, and struck an attitude, still laughing. Then his laughter stopped. My friend had shoved a revolver against his left eye, and I was saying:

"Move an inch or utter a sound, and I swear that you will never leave alive." He froze. "Your safe," I said. "Open up your safe immediately — and don't move!"

He shook his head. My friend said: "I watched him yesterday. As we left he took a key from around his neck. That's where he always keeps it, I expect."

I thrust my hand under the gold coat, under waistcoat, shirt, and undervest. There hung a little heavy key. "Hold him. Keep him silent," I said; for I knew that coward as he was, Potdevin was also a miser, who valued gold above his blood and his life. His safe, I knew, would be near where he slept. I went to the bedroom at the back of the shop. The safe was there. I took only paper money and bonds, to the tune of three million francs ... and perhaps I picked up a jewel or two. I forget. Then I returned and opened the shop door. "Ready," I said to my friend; and as he released Potdevin, we both rushed into the street screaming "*Aidez–nous! Au secours!*"

A gendarme was walking about, a hundred yards away. He turned as we rushed towards him. Just then, roaring like seven bulls, Potdevin came bounding out, waving the dreadful–looking Malay sword. The play was going precisely to schedule.

"Lunatic! Lunatic!" I shouted, and ran towards the place where our car was waiting — a powerful Panhard, as fast as anything that existed then. The gendarme hesitated: Potdevin was an awful figure in his helmet and his silks, and with his wavy blade flashing. My friend reached the car. I ran ten yards behind him. The gendarme threw himself on Potdevin, and they struggled, hand–and–heel together. "Thieves, thieves!" shrieked Potdevin, while the gendarme hung on to his wrist. He was a strong fellow, that ginger villain: he pushed the policeman aside, and came after me.

And then a dreadful thing happened. I slipped and fell. I heard Potdevin's feet pounding up; rose to one knee. Then he was upon me. I was overcome, and slightly stunned. I saw his red face, mad with rage, and the hunch of his shoulder as he drew back the sword. There was murder in his eyes. I threw myself sideways, and glimpsed my friend, the good fellow, coming back, revolver in hand. And at that moment there was a shattering bang near my left ear, and I saw Potdevin drop his sword and clasp his chest. "My friend has fired," I thought, and rose. The gendarme was there. He was saying "Brave girl." Girl? I swung round, wondering what had happened.

Standing there, with a smoking shotgun protruding from a smouldering parcel, stood the girl of Ostende, like a haggard Nemesis. And Potdevin was very, very dead ...

Karmesin sighed, and put his shoes down side by side. I blinked at him. There seemed a few untidy ends to his story. He answered my unspoken queries.

"We told the police how Potdevin had pursued us out into the street, under a delusion that he was the King of Siam. The gendarme bore witness. The girl had the sense to keep her mouth shut, and was even commended for her prompt action ... you know how it is, in France. We got away quickly that night ..."

"And the girl?" That was a question I could not refrain from putting.

"Ah, what is the use?" said Karmesin. "I sent her a hundred thousand francs."

"And what did she do?" Again the query was irrepressible.

"Opened a questionable house in Lille, and made a fortune," said Karmesin. "But all the same, seven *is* a mysterious number ..."

Chickenfeed for Karmesin

God, how I was singing! At the top of my voice. I rummaged in my repertoire for something which would enable me to let myself go; picked on "Celeste Aïda," and let it out in a bellow. "Celeste Aïda," I sang, "Ce–leste Aï–daaaaaaaa. Ce–lest–te A–i–daaaaa. Celeste A–hi–daaaaaaa. Wow. *Celeste* Aï —"

"Shut up," said Karmesin. "Anyway, what is all the noise about? Why do you sing? I mean, why do you try to sing? You have a voice like the noise of a lockmaker's workshop. There is a jail in Pau where they have a rusty lock. When the turnkey locks you in, it sounds just like that. So be so kind as to shut up. Have you a cigarette? *What's* this? *Sacré nom du marché parallèle!*"

I had thrown over a packet. Karmesin was looking at it as if he could not believe the evidence of his eyes. He gaped. His nostrils twitched in anticipatory zest.

"What *is* this?" he said again, "twenty cigarettes? Real cigarettes at twenty for two–and–four? For the love of God stop singing, my friend."

I stopped. Karmesin had already taken five cigarettes out of the packet. "Noise Tax," he said, pocketing four. "Have you a match?"

"Or would you prefer a cigar?" I asked.

"*What* is all this?" asked Karmesin.

I unclenched my right hand and showed him ten pounds in cash. His self–control was admirable. He picked up the notes, looked at them to see if they were genuine.

I stopped singing, and said, "You know that story you told me — about the way you robbed a bank in the Strand? I wrote it down and sold it."

Karmesin became black in the face. "You rat," he said, "you despicable animal! *Fetiuk! Pfui* on you, you *hijo de puta*, you — you reptile! Species of camel, *va!* Breaker of confidences! *Himmelherrgottkreutzmillionendonnerwetter* and blast! I will break your legs! How much did you get for it?"

"Ten guineas. Take a pound out of it."

"Ten filthy dirty miserable guineas! You sold your soul — I mean *my* soul — for that! And now you are generous. Ha, ha! You cut off my tail, eat the meat, and give me the bones. *Pfui!* You take the skin off my back and generously return me my shirt. *Hoo!* You eat up my oyster and then make a gesture by offering me the shell. *Ekh–ma!* You sell *my* birthright for a mess of pottage. Ha, a generous fellow. He would give you the shirt off his best friend's back. Oh, very nice, very nice. I will not take your pound. Ten guineas. Oof! ... Why didn't you ask twenty–five?"

"They wouldn't have paid it."

"But you could have asked. But no. You slink into the office, and say 'Oh, please' and 'Oh, thank you,' you worm of worms."

"They have a standard rate of pay."

"You should have demanded more. But. But. But, always but. I know. You wanted the money. Fool, you should have pretended not to want the money. You should have turned it over with your walking stick and said '*Pfui.*'"

"Are you taking this pound or not?" I waved one of the notes at him.

"I am magnanimous. I give it to you. Your story, after all."

"But you deserve at least ten per cent commission."

"My young friend, am I a commission–agent? No. Keep your money. I have only worked on commission once, and that was not, I assure you, for such despicable chickenfeed. I will not take your pound. I will, if you wish, borrow it. But as commission? No. Never shall it be said that Karmesin betrayed a confidence."

"Then borrow it," I said, "and tell me about your commission."

"Not for publication. Give me your word of honour. Very well," said Karmesin, "buy my tea and I will tell you. And a cigar. I want a cigar. A three–and–sixpenny cigar. That is all I will take from you. The pound is only a loan ..."

The only time I ever consented to work on a commission basis (said Karmesin) was not very long ago, and I made a hundred and seventy–five thousand pounds. It was the simplest deal of my life. I may have mentioned that I am a genius. This was genius. Only I did not make that respectable sum of money by grabbing in an undignified way after dirty, measly, niggardly sums of guineas. No.

I can imagine your beady little pig's eyes popping out of your head, eh? Bah to you! Say somebody laid down on this table before you five thousand pounds in notes? What would you do? You would scream like a stuck hog and fix your grubby little hands into it. No? Yes. One day I shall teach you the value of self-denial.

But I am not like that. As an operative in any business, I always played for big money. The chickenfeed, the dirty little hundreds and thousands, I threw aside. Let smaller men scramble for such handfuls of maize. I, Karmesin, play high. So.

You must know that I have a world-wide reputation as a man who can do, or arrange to have done, practically anything under the sun. If you wanted a new president elected in an obscure State, you would only have to come to me, and lay down a sum of money, and say, "Karmesin, do me the honour to arrange the small matter ..." I am a fixer. I have a peculiar charm. I can penetrate to any place on earth, from a pigsty to a palace. Kings have availed themselves of my universal contacts. Queens have had occasion to thank their lucky stars for my cold, clear brain which burns like a star, and for my nerves of steel, and for my will which is like a rock. As for my discretion, it is proverbial. I never talk. Red-hot knives would not cut information out of me. Now listen, for I am giving you the inside dope on a great deal which took place in the very early 1920's. Post-war periods are all more or less alike, the best time for men like me.

I was in Paris, staying, as was usual, at the most exclusive and luxurious hotel in the city. I had a little money about me, but only very little. I had not been working, and had been amusing myself in no uncertain manner. They will still tell you, in Bucharest, how I bathed a whole cabaret in the finest champagne. A fact! One bath-tub each, full to the brim. And I had to import the bath-tubs, too. But that is all nothing. I was at the ... let us say, the Hotel Behemoth. It is a haunt of kings and diplomats. The beds you sleep on have given rest to the noblest bones in the world. And sometimes, in the bath, you may find, clinging near the taps, a hair from an ambassador. It was at the Behemoth that Julie Delamimi kicked the Ruritanian Prime Minister in the face and broke all his bridge-work. The pieces were scattered all over the grill room.

Well, listen. Staying at the Behemoth at the same time as I, was a certain illustrious personage. He was from the Balkans, and had the dark, sinister air of all Balkan potentates. I had better not mention his name: it is a great one. I am discreet.

We met one evening at the American Bar. He was slightly drunk and clamouring for a Thunderbird Cocktail — an obscure and unheard-of cocktail of incredible potency, of which only three men on earth know the recipe. (I am one of these three.) Barney, the barman, was nonplussed. I came to the rescue. Soon, we got into conversation. The Illustrious Personage had heard of me. He had heard my name in connection with the Mexican oil deal that so shocked the Paris Bourse. You remember ...

Soon, we were friendly. I dined with him. He dined with me. Then he opened his heart. My friend, I open hearts as other men open tomato-cans. He told me that he was on a species of trade mission. He had to buy some rifles. That should have been easy enough; but there was a hitch.

His government had entrusted him with four hundred thousand pounds in cash. He had done away with over a hundred thousand. How, he didn't quite know. Certainly, he had had a dream about Number Nine, and had done mad things with heavy money at Monte Carlo. Again, half the ballet dancers in Paris had broken out in diamonds as if it were a rash. In a word, he had only about three hundred thousand pounds left with which to buy £400,000 worth of guns, and wanted help. His credit, I may say, stank. Besides, he wanted the matter hushed up. He wanted to do a bit of fixing — £10,000 here, £10,000 there, and so get away with £400,000 in goods at the price of about £250,000. He was prepared to pay £250,000 in cash. But who would help him?

I said, "My young friend, be easy. It is as good as settled. I know everybody concerned. Meet me tomorrow at six, and we can arrange it all."

That night I made enquiries. By the following day at midday, I was in possession of certain essential personal details about the men whom he was due to meet. When I saw the Illlustrious Personage, I had the whole story at my fingertips. I could get him his arms for a couple of hundred thousand, cash. "£25,000 will satisfy me, just for the deal," I said. He took out a bundle of notes as thick as a plum–cake.

"No," I said. "Don't pay me now. Pay me afterwards. After the deal goes through satisfactorily, pay me then." He was delighted. At last he had found an honest man. I added. "But Mr. So–and–so (naming a very highly–placed government official) will want about £75,000 for his share in the deal." Out came the roll again. I pooh–poohed it. "No," I said. "He must wait, as I am doing. He must not get a penny until everything is satisfactorily concluded, and your goods are shipped."

It is here, my idiotic young friend, that you would have spoiled everything, by going blue about the gills and seizing all the money in sight. But me? £75,000? *Pfui!*

We arranged that he should meet me at the Hotel Mastodon in Park Lane on January 5, and I went away. Is there significance in the date? My young friend! No, just verisimilitude. You will never get anywhere without a mind like a card–index system.

Now it so happened that, by some means which I was never able to trace, a word leaked through to the English police. Scotland Yard instantly nosed after the affair. They simply discovered that my illustrious friend was due to meet me in London on the fifth. They waited for him. He was flying over. A couple of very amiable detectives met his Excellency as the plane descended, and asked him who he was. They looked at his passport, and their foreheads touched the ground. Then they asked him if he had any money with him. "Yes," he said, producing his wallet. They counted his wad, and turned pale. Their hands shook as they returned the money.

"You must leave the country at once," they said to him. Protest was useless. You know what the English police are; you cannot argue with them. The plane took my friend back, and I was slightly worried. Had he been dragged out of my fingers, just as everything was all right? But no. I reassured myself. And not in vain. Three days later, I received a message. He was back in England. He had chartered a special launch to land him on the coast, and had made his way to London. And so we met, as arranged, at the Mastodon, and sat down to drink a cognac and talk.

"It is all arranged," I told him.

"Do you give your friend his £75,000?" he asked, producing his wallet.

"No," I said, very firmly, "it must be when everything is perfectly satisfactory."

"Then do, at least, please take your £25,000."

"Afterwards," I said. "When the matter is arranged."

"I have never met such a man," he said, in delight, "I shall have you decorated with the Order of Saint Sapphira, First Class. I shall also have you made a baron."

"I am honoured," I said. Notice how calm I remained.

"Are you sure you won't have that £25,000 now?" I shook my head decisively. "As you wish," he said. "What must I do?"

"Pay for the goods, and then have them delivered without delay. I can help you arrange delivery. I can then with an easy conscience take my commission."

"Will you pay?" he asked. "I shall feel happier if you do."

"As you wish," I said, "Perhaps you'll feel better if you do it yourself."

"No, no." — "Yes, yes." — "No, no." — "Yes, yes." — "No, no."

"No, I insist," he said. "My dear, dear friend, I insist."

"Very well," I replied, with a shrug, and took the £175,000 which he handed me, and I cleared out, and that is the end of the story.

Karmesin finished his tea with a terrible whooping noise. I said: "Really, I don't believe that. There are many reasons for not believing that — one hundred and seventy-five thousand — and on nothing but your word ..."

"Who cares about that?" said Karmesin. "Remember, I had a reputation for financial and commercial wizardry. Again, confidence was created by my refusing huge sums of money. Whether you believe it or not, it is true. You can ask any crime reporter on the newspapers, or any inspector at Scotland Yard if this is not a true story. They all know I did it. But no charge was laid against me, and so I could never be touched as a consequence of it. This tea is terrible. England drinks the dregs of the tea crop. Really," he mimicked, "I shall have to look into Mincing Lane and tell them ..."

"And what did you do with the money?" I asked.

"The £175,000? Can I remember every penny I spend? God knows. I forget," said Karmesin, surreptitiously filling his waistcoat pockets with sugar.

The Thief Who Played Dead

Karmesin's moustache has always fascinated me. It is full of zoological interest; it appears to live a life of its own. When I first met him twenty–five years ago, it resembled a hibernating squirrel. Ten years later, it had turned into a dying raccoon. And now it was a grey–backed gull seeking refuge from a storm under the jutting crag of his formidable nose, so that as his cigarette burned down low I half expected it to fly away with a terrible squawk. But he rescued it in the nick of time, dropped the glowing stub into the dregs of his coffee cup, and gave it a reassuring pat.

He caught my glance — Karmesin missed nothing — and said: "Yes, old boy, it has gone white. It grew out white after I shaved it off in 1923."

"For a disguise?" I asked.

"Well, to lay the foundations for one. Ah, that was an affair! The world has never seen the like of it, and never will again!"

Now Karmesin is an enigma. In all the years I have known him, I have never been able to decide whether he is the greatest criminal, or the greatest liar, the world has ever known. Either way, he is great. He has his facts at his fingertips — the unlikeliest facts. He never contradicts himself, and when he falls into a reminiscent mood he casts such a spell upon you by a kind of sleight–of–mind that, while he talks, you must believe ... He is the conjurer and you, the child at the party when, in the dimmed light, the bowl of goldfish comes out of the hat. And you go away saying to yourself: *It must be a lie ... Or was it?*

"Tell me about it," I said.

With heavy sarcasm, he said: "There is no earthly use telling you anything, you. You never believe me. You are one of those fools that call themselves 'sceptics,' and 'hard–headed,' et cetera, et cetera. And what fools you turn out to be in your misbelief! You will believe in Signor Ponzi's gold, or Ivar Kreugar's mad promises, far more sincerely than you believe in God. That is why the easiest money I have ever made has been by picking out the shrewdest sceptic I could find."

"Oh, Karmesin!" I begged.

"I will tell you, briefly," said Karmesin with a chuckle, "just in order to shock you ..."

Oh, if I could convey to you that sonorous, steady, insistent, hypnotic voice of Karmesin's when he began to talk, gazing straight in front of him! And his eyes. You have seen one of those ancient portraits in which the subject, looking at nothing, appears from every angle to be watching you? Such were the eyes of Karmesin, as he told his story ...

I am that rare combination, a thinker and a man of action (Karmesin began). Therefore, it has been possible for me, in the course of a long life devoted almost exclusively to robbery in most of its forms, to conceive and execute some of the most sensational coups in the history of crime. But what I am going to tell you constitutes the history of, perhaps, the most audacious and spectacular robbery of all time.

It also involves a discovery which, if published, would shake the world. It would drive news of a world catastrophe on to Page Three. And as for the loot, well, the man who had that in his pocket — if he had come by it honestly — could command anything. Magnates would cry for it; nations would bid for it; treasuries would be ransacked for the purchase of it — if it had been honestly come by. Even now, hundreds of thousands would be paid for the return of it, if only one knew where to find it. And believe me, it is hard to find, because it is nothing but a tattered scrap of half-rotten vellum that you could cover with one hand, scribbled with seventy-five broken words on one side, and some crabbed dog-Latin on the other. I was paid two million dollars for stealing it.

You want to know who paid me two million dollars, and for exactly what? Aha, my boy, here we come to the privileged classes, the higher ups! I may not mention real names for fear that you might repeat them to your own destruction — for I, most certainly, on inquiry would deny all knowledge of this affair.

There are, as you must know, dynasties of dollars: Hamburger II, Limburger IV, Van Elbow VI, and so on. All right, my pay came from a hereditary magnate of the third generation whom I will call Mr. Three.

His grandfather was a species of Dr. Moriarty of high finance ... a sort of arachnid in a tenuous web. He begot a son, who was the worst of the lot, and so the fortune descended to Mr. Three. Now there — God save the Queen! — there was a strange one. Although he had been brought up to great expectations, he had been grudgingly shoved through college until, having acquired a master's degree in the arts, he became a teacher. Brother, I have studied under hard masters, but the Lord preserve me from such a one as Three must have been! I have some little experience of him. He was a spy, a watcher-by-night, a pedant of the most learned sort. There was no way of having Mr. Three.

I was introduced to him by a man named Sweetbread, and this man was, in his way, one of the most sinister characters I have ever encountered. He was an agent for Mr. Three.

But before I go on: another word about Mr. Three. He had a hundred million dollars, but lived at the rate of about twelve dollars a week in a brownstone house that might have been magnificent if he had kept it clean.

He did not smoke: for him tobacco was dust and ashes, catarrh and halitosis — and so many dollars chucked into the ashtrays. He informed me, with some severity, that the stump of a Corona-Corona which, in a moment of impatience, I discarded in his presence; was in point of fact worth five dollars and seven cents, if I counted taxes.

Alcohol he abhorred, clothes he regarded as vanity; he went about shabby as only a multi-millionaire dare afford to be. As for women: Mr. Three was afraid of them.

Mr. Three, born a millionaire and a miser, became a collector. It is the same thing, in effect. As a numismatist collects gold coins because they are old or *recherché*, so any other kind of collector, turning specie into the worth of it, gathers and grasps — whether it be metal or stone, or (which is most valuable) paper in the form of books, etchings, stamps and what-not.

In point of fact, these wretches of collectors are worse than penurious. Your common or garden miser grabs hard cash, and holds it until God strikes him dead. He deals only in dirty money. But your collector of the fine arts makes blind alleys into which run the works of great men. I could always rob such types with an easy conscience.

However, much as I hated and despised Mr. Three for his vile greed, I detested Sweetbread even more. He was an M.A., an Oxford man; something of a lecturer; a bit of a critic; an eccentric. Oh, what a repulsive man he was, with his greenish fish-belly face, and his horrid, fruity, liver–coloured mouth that was never quite wet or dry, and made a tiny, sticky, smacking sound every time it opened!

Yet a scholar, mark you, a man of erudition!

Tortuous in his ways, serpentine in his means, armed with one of the best brains in England, Sweetbread went in pursuit of that which was out of the way. His was a clammy passion, a grave–robber's love for what lay buried; a desire to disturb that which was supposed to be at rest.

Now one evening, he came to me and said: "M. Karmesin, would you be interested in a million dollars or so?"

"Perhaps," I said.

"I have a billionaire," said Sweetbread, "ripe for a bite."

"Oh?"

"It is legitimate," Sweetbread said, using sporting jargon, which came unpleasantly out of his mouth. "Play or pay. Deliver or nothing. You understand? Only out of the grand total, I must have one–quarter, which might run as high as half a million dollars."

"Aie, aie, aie!" I said. "Here, in effect, is a bite!"

"Indeed," said Sweetbread. "The bite of bites! Better meet my principal."

And so I did.

Mr. Three said to Sweetbread: "You have, no doubt, explained the matter to this gentleman?"

"No, Mr. Three, I have not," said Sweetbread. "Not without, your permission. It is a delicate matter, I think."

"Then I will thank you kindly to explain," said Mr. Three. At this point, Sweetbread became academic. He gave me an interesting mixture of fact and conjecture, the gist of which was as follows:

The poet, Edmund Spenser, died in 1599, and was buried in Westminster Abbey. Now as far as I am concerned, the author of *The Faerie Queen* is one of the most ponderous and prodigious bores in Elizabethan literature. Yet he earned the affection of his Queen, and therefore received certain outward signs of respect from his betters. So, when Edmund Spenser died, there was a show of grief.

When he was buried, the greatest of his contemporaries wrote poems to throw into his grave. And, when I give you their names, you will observe that in the grave of Edmund Spenser were buried manuscripts more precious than the Codex Siniaticus.

There were present Michael Drayton, Thomas Nashe, John Donne, Ben Jonson, and William Shakespeare. Every one of these great Elizabethans cast into Spenser's grave a poem specially written for the occasion of his burial.

William Shakespeare was thirty-five years old at the time, and engaged upon a pot-boiler entitled *Much Ado About Nothing*. He was in the middle of it when Edmund Spenser had to come home from Ireland and die!

Sweetbread said that, according to his conjecture, it was Michael Drayton — a gentle, sentimental little busybody of a minor poet who went bursting about London, collaring the greatest literary figures of the time and, with womanish persistence, nagging and worrying them away from their business until they wrote mourning verses to be dropped with a decent show of grief into old Edmund Spenser's coffin.

That the poets I have mentioned finally did so, is historical fact. I fancy that the eager beaver, Michael Drayton, got at Ben Jonson first, in the Mermaid Tavern, and, having mellowed him with a double-quart of sherry, talked him into promising to write a few lines in honour of the author of *The Faerie Queene*.

Then, in the time-honoured manner of such well-meaning but persistent pests, he went to Shakespeare and said, in effect: "I hope I am not disturbing you, Will, but Ben has pledged his word to write a bit of an ode for poor Edmund. I am turning out a little sonnet myself, in my own poor way. How about you?"

Whereupon, William Shakespeare, unwilling to offend Drayton and Jonson, two tried old friends, pushed aside the tedious manuscript of *Much Ado About Nothing*, and, taking up a scrap of vellum, dashed off what was for him, a very poor sonnet.

Ah, naturally you ask me how Sweetbread knew that it was a scrap of vellum and a sonnet.

Well, Sweetbread did not know. He knew only the bare historical facts. It was I who discovered the details, as I am about to tell you. Briefly: Mr. Three made it clear that he would pay two million dollars, and no questions asked, for that original manuscript of William Shakespeare.

Here, if you like, was something of a tall order! I ask you: walk into Westminster Abbey, open one of the famous graves, rummage in it and walk out undetected. Just try it and see!

I said to Mr. Three: "No doubt, if I were prepared to risk my liberty, you, would be prepared to chance a little money in advance?"

Upon this, there was a sordid haggling; but in the end (acquainted with my reputation for scrupulous fair-dealing) Mr. Three agreed to advance me fifty thousand dollars, and to put down a certified cheque payable on a date which I will call the twenty-third.

It was on this date that I guaranteed to deliver whatever manuscripts I might find in the tomb of Edmund Spenser — especially the Shakespeare manuscript. Thus, upon a precarious understanding, I went to work at one of the trickiest jobs in the history of crime, working on a hunch.

Now, exactly why did I pin myself down to this date in particular? I will tell you. Two days before this date, on the twenty-first, workmen were due to enter the Abbey in order to make certain repairs.

Simply, I proposed to join them. And so I did, and thus I carried away, for two million dollars, an original manuscript of William Shakespeare.

But how?

... There was a time, my boy, when I used to attend the annual meeting of the Conjurers' Club — myself an amateur — when the leading magicians of the country demonstrated to one another their newest tricks.

One evening, at one of these meetings, a group of five Yorkshiremen dressed as Chinamen walked on and off the stage, putting up an open tent. They went, they came; they came, and they went. This one carried a pole; that one carried a flag; another dragged a carpet; a fourth shouldered a mallet; the fifth stood still in a mandarin's robe and did nothing. They came, they went — never leaving that little stage. But all of a sudden, the little tent being twitched away, there were only four Chinamen. One — two — three — four: categorically four Chinamen only.

They bustled about, picking up pegs, rolling up canvas, fetching and carrying (never leaving the stage) and then, there were two!

Rolled up in the tent, you guess? Not so. The man carrying the canvas let it unroll and fall with a terrible thud. Still, only two Chinamen left out of five, on a bare stage, with no backdrops, mirrors, or other apparatus. Three men spirited away, ha?

This trick I saw through, and remembered. It's a very old one. Let anyone grow accustomed to your comings and goings, especially if you are carrying something, and you remain unnoticeable. As simple as that! In the magician's trick, one person, the mandarin, stood stock-still. Upon him all eyes were concentrated. His four collaborators came and went, and so, under the keenest eyes in the world could go without coming again, and still, in the imagination of the audience, remain present.

Hypnosis of stillness? That is well enough in its place. But for general purposes, give me the hypnosis of coming-and-going. A combination of the two is difficult to resist.

So I dyed my moustache red and applied to my forehead a lock of hair such as is called a "quiff."

Then I dressed myself in working man's clothes, took hold of a plank, and went with the others into the Abbey; bustled up and down with crowbars and wedges. When in doubt, keep moving as if with a set purpose.

An official looked at me questioningly, once; but, pulling out of my pocket a cold chisel, I shouted: "All right, all right, all right — I'm coming, Jack" — and so disappeared as two men passed me with a thing like a hospital stretcher loaded with concrete.

As often as possible, I carried bulky objects on my shoulder just in case, in passing, someone chanced to take too keen an interest in my face. I had a bad moment when the foreman accosted me, and said "Hoi! Who are you? What the hell have you got there?"

But I am a man who has made a habit of anticipating the Unexpected, and foreseeing the Unforeseen. I had, as a matter of routine, found out the name of the foreman, and the names of his immediate superiors.

"Cement, Mr. Edwards," I said, letting fall the sack. "Mr. Graves sent me. He said you was a man short."

He said, with a kind of weary disgust: "I don't know nothing about that. Oh well, all right. Got your card and pass, I suppose? Well, get cracking, Jumbo, and lend a hand with that mortar. Mix, man, mix! We haven't got all day ..."

They had not, indeed — there was little time to go before the gang stopped work for the day. But I was annoyed at being recognized as a stranger. My plan originally had been to pass entirely unnoticed; to hide myself in the shadows when the workmen went out, taking my bits of paper at my leisure; and so, out, with a ladder on my shoulder when they came back next morning.

But now I had swiftly to change my plan. I had to stay conspicuous under the very eyes of the foreman and yet remain invisible.

As usual, I had an inspiration, one of my little flashes of genius. Now any silly sedentary thriller-writer may perpetrate or detect from an armchair, but it takes a man of action with nerves of steel to do what I did then. Slipping into the shadows, I stripped myself of shoes, trousers, and shirt, so that I stood in my underclothes. People have sometimes laughed at me for wearing combinations, or a union-suit, as it is also called. I can tell you, I was glad of that union-suit then. I dipped both hands into a bag of cement which I had placed in readiness, and whitened myself from head to foot.

Then I lay down on the blank surface of a plain tomb, crossed my arms, and kept still. There was only half an hour to go before the whistle blew, but that half-hour was one of the most trying I have ever spent in my life.

My nostrils were full of cement so that I wanted to sneeze, and I itched abominably. Once, I heard the foreman say: "Where's that big slob got to now? The one Graves sent?"

One of the workmen said: "Dunno, gaffer. Thought I see 'im lugging a plank, a little while back."

So he had; but time is a tricky thing when you are on a job and haven't got a watch.

"I'm fed up with the loafers Graves sends me ... All right, knock off now. Go home, and eat your sausages and kippers — that's all you're fit for. Pack up!"

One of the workmen naively tried to tell him that *his* wife made him a nice meat pie for his tea ... and there I lay straining every muscle to hold back a monumental sneeze. Thank heaven the lights were being switched out! — for, as they passed me, two of the workmen stopped to look at me.

One of them said: "Who's he, Jack? Never noticed that image before."

"You wouldn't," said the other with contempt. "It's some famous poet. Bin dead a thousand years. Where's yer education?"

"It ain't even life–like," his companion said. "Sort of in'uman, ain't it?"

"Kind of gruesome. But, p'r'aps, they looked like that in olden times ... Let's get out of 'ere, they're shutting up."

I do not know whether this was the greatest compliment, or the deadliest insult, I have ever received. It added to my discomfort, however, because in addition to that maddening urge to sneeze, I had a wild impulse to cry, in a sepulchral voice: *"Boo!"* and this impulse gave rise to a terrible desire to laugh.

But they went their ways, and at last I was alone.

The rest was easy, if somewhat ghoulish. The Abbey, as you know, is patrolled by watchmen. Having ascertained the times of their coming and going, I could go to work at my leisure. And so I did, with crowbars and wedges.

I was glad that the remains of poor Edmund Spenser were encased in lead, and that the poets had dropped their offerings on top of the casket. Thus, it was not necessary for me to disturb his dust. In the light of my flash–lamp I saw, lying on that leaden surface, some detritus that might once have been paper, but now resembled (let us say) cornflakes. The vellum alone remained, and that only in part. So, I took it; and with all reverence, sealed the tomb ...

Oh, but that was a long, cold night I spent hiding in the shadows among the graves! But the night passed, and when the workmen came back I was among them in my labourer's clothes, having washed myself in a pail of water that was used to make mortar. There I was, carrying a shovel.

The foreman shouted at me: "You lump! You blithering gowk! Where did you get to yesterday evening?"

"I had a stomach ache."

"Well, take your stomach ache out of here. Take it to Mr. Graves, and tell him I don't want you. I'll pick my own gangs, by the Lord —"

And so I got away with that priceless bit of vellum, for which, true to his word, Mr. Three paid me two million dollars; of which I duly handed half a million to Sweetbread.

There is the story.

"Well," said Karmesin, "you will not believe even such a straightforward story as that now, I suppose?"

I said, in mollifying tones: "After all, Karmesin, such a story is hard to credit without, say, a bit of documentary evidence."

He was not perturbed, as I had feared he might be. "Documentary evidence? But, of course," he said, pulling out of an inside pocket the biggest wallet I have ever seen. "Let me see, now ...? Let me see ..."

He took out a piece of stiff paper about six inches by four and, offering it to me, said: "Here you are. Before I handed over the original, I made a photographic copy. Can you read it?"

I could not decipher more than a word or two. I saw, simply, a couple of detached rags of an old manuscript, but I could read the signature — *William Shakspere*.

"May I have a copy of this?" I asked.

"No, you may not," said Karmesin. "But, if you like, I will rewrite you these lines, as Sweetbread transcribed them in modern spelling."

He took pencil and paper, and here is what I, in my turn, pass on:

... 'nd Spenser
Would that with these poor words
I seal'd my grief
In this cold grave, old friend. Yet
mourn I must
For memory runs more slower
than the thief
That men call Death, and when
these bones are dust
Since grief like noble wine grows
strong and sweet
With Time in shadow, so my
mourning will.
(Lines missing here.)

God grant that you sleep deep while
we who wake
And born to be forgot await our
Night.
     William Shakspere.

"Shakespeare did better," said Karmesin, putting back the wallet. "But remember, at that time, he was harassed with show business, and the script of *Much Ado About Nothing*."

"But," I said, "since the existence of these manuscripts in Spenser's tomb was known, why hasn't the government investigated?"

Karmesin said: "It has. Acting on irrefutable evidence, the grave of Edmund Spenser was officially opened in 1938. Consult your authorities, if you don't believe me. They opened the grave, and found nothing. I had been there first, you see."

"But the manuscript, the manuscript!" I cried.

Karmesin said: "Ah, that. Pity. Mr. Three married a frugal house wife in 1929; someone after his own heart, more or less. He died not long after. I rather think that a sympathetic collector of unconsidered trifles got hold of the Shakespeare manuscript. I know for a fact that a dealer named Newgate paid an absurd price — ten times collector's value — for a first edition of *Tom Jones*, 'With Miscellaneous Papers, Etcetera,' and, in the spring of 1931, bought a yacht."

"It all seems so incredible," I said.

"I am tired of your 'incredibles.' Why, only the other day a few Scottish amateurs walked into Westminster Abbey, and trotted out with the sacred Stone of Scone, upon which the throne of England stands. Their trick was the same as mine, old as the hills. Child's play. I should not have troubled to mention my little affair, except that I know you to be interested in literary curiosities. Thanks for the lunch. Au revoir."

The Conscience of Karmesin

Karmesin, who, if he is not the greatest criminal of all time, must certainly be the most perfect liar the world has ever known, said to me: "It is a convention of the journalists to say that burglary is the most underpaid profession in the world. *Tfoo* to that!"

"What do you mean, *tfoo*?" I asked. "It stands to reason —"

"— I know, I know. Counting the time your average burglar spends in jail, what with one thing and another, his earnings work out at somewhat less than a street-sweeper may rely upon for honest labour. And he has no Union to fall back on, either. Aha, yes! Here, you speak of your *average* burglar. You might as well say: *Writers end in the gutter.* Generally, they do. But did Dickens? Did Thackeray? Did Tennyson? I do not observe Mr. James Hadley Chase grinding a barrel-organ, or Mr. Spillane lining up for soup. Do you? No. Your master craftsman will make his way, believe me!

" 'Average' is as much as to say 'Mediocrity'. Speak for yourself, Kersh," said Karmesin, brushing a kind of foggy dew off his moustache, which the inclemency of the weather had turned anti-clockwise, while he fished out a waistcoat-pocket a gnarled old cigarette. "Given Ethics, be a thief. Only never abandon your Ethics!"

When I began to protest, Karmesin exclaimed: "Oh, *ptoo*!" Then, casually: "Ever heard about the greatest robbery of all time?"

"Every five minutes," I said.

"I committed it," said Karmesin. "Only it did not pay on account of Ethics. Listen to me and I will tell you why."

This was by way of being an intellectual exercise, rather than a major operation; because if I got away with that which I set out to get, there would have been little profit for me and a considerable amount of loss. Not loss of money. Not even much loss of liberty, since I have never had a criminal record, never having been convicted.

No, no, I should have suffered a leakage of the morale, a loss of *amour proper*, and that would have been the end of Karmesin. Understand this: what I did was not for money; it was for its own sake. I was by no means short of a few hundred pounds, having recently got away with the Knoblock Emeralds. Even so I found myself sitting in an hotel which shall be nameless, wondering what to do with myself.

I could tell you a dozen stories of what I proposed to do, about then; and nothing satisfied me. At last, I came across a note from an Argentinian who has written to me some years before, asking me to visit him.

This man's name, let us say, was Tombola, and he was a 'cattle king.' Where even Texans count their steers, Tombola counted his cowboys. Nothing Tombola did could possibly go wrong. He had cows, so he sold the meat; he had beeves, so he made capital out of the hides; he had hooves — he made glue, or calf's foot jelly, or invalid food, or goodness knows what. Every horn and bone of his beasts yielded a handle for a shaving brush made out of their bristles. He did not know what to do with his money. Everything came his way.

He was a character, this 'King' Tombola. Only, a megalomaniac: he had more than he knew what to do with. Hence, quite seriously, when I visited him, he made me a proposition. He was in a state of frustration, having failed in an attempt to gold-plate a white Arab stallion. The horse died.

To cut a long story short, he said this: "They call me 'King' Tombola. Where's my crown? ... Have one made, you say? No, thank you! I want a real one, a proper one. I have been offered the crown of the Incas, and all that truck. I want a crown of the King of England, nothing less. I will pay seven million dollars in gold for it."

This gave me food for thought. Resisting 'King' Tombola's invitation to bathe, that night, in a hipbath of green chartreuse, I left next day for England to steal the Crown Jewels.

... To steal the Crown Jewels, as you may be informed, is impossible, nowadays. They were lifted, once, by Colonel Thomas Blood on May 9th, 1671. But this affair was juvenile delinquent stuff.

Having obtained access to the Crown Jewels, it was necessary, simply, for Colonel Blood to overpower the Keeper of the Regalia — an old gentleman of eighty. I ask you — obtain access through a rabble of superannuated halberdiers, and spifflicate your grandfather! Even so,

Colonel Blood was caught, running away with the Crown of England under his cloak. The Merry Monarch, amused by Blood's audacity — the audacity of a little boy stealing a packet of chewing gum from a drugstore — pardoned him.

But, between 1671 and 1939, when I stole the Crown Jewels, two hundred and sixty-eight years had passed, and circumstances were not the same.

Today, the Crown Jewels are protected by unbreakable glass and a two-inch grille of the toughest steel; I say 'unbreakable', as it were, in the commercial sense of the term, which really means 'more than ordinarily hard to chuck a brick through.' You could burn your way through the steel and the glass that guard the Crown Jewels, yes; but, do you know what would happen when you did so?

You would break a series of electric circuits. There would be a tintinnabulation to raise the devil. The Yeomen of the Guard would rush out. The River Police would fly to the spot in their fast little boats from up and down the Thames. The Brigade of Guards would be there, with fixed bayonets. The Flying Squad would be on the spot in a matter of minutes.

This is not all. Certain other electric currents would automatically close and seal all the doors of the Jewel Room, while the platform that holds the Jewels would be electrically drawn down, out of sight and out of reach.

Of all the jobs in the world, as I calculate, three are impossible: and the greatest of these impossibilities is to steal the Crown Jewels.

I stole them, of course; but, first, I had to choose a time, and make a plan. A plan any fool can make: indeed, most of the fools I have known have come to grief by their plans. Show me the man who can choose his time, and I will show you a man of genius; and when I speak of timing, I do not mean the picking of a month, or the choosing of a week, or even the selection of an hour — I mean, getting between the finger-and-thumb of a diagnostic intellect one microscopic crumb of operative time, the one and only instant.

Leave it to me to find the instant. In this instant I perpetrated the most stupendous robbery of all time, my friend. It is now necessary for me to go, briefly, into a little psychology; even, if you like, a bit of metaphysics and international politics.

England, by the year 1939, was in a certain predicament for which it is difficult to find a metaphor. Say, if you like, that she had taken to heart too much of the philosophy of those three popular 'wise' monkeys. You know them, these apes? The British Government, at the time of which I speak, had fallen into a deplorably 'wise' monkeyfied habit. She saw no Mussolini, heard no Hitler, spoke no Franco, and smelled no Stalin — never in history has there been such a Belshazzar's Feast of illiterates who could not read the Handwriting on the Wall! There was a European Situation — and how! as the Americans say.

The term 'Fifth Column' had passed into the English language. A convenient term for provocation, espionage, sabotage, and treachery, it had become as familiar to the man in the street as the name of Judas Iscariot. For example, Hitler's agents were assisting what there was left of the old Irish Republican Army, working in Belfast and Dublin. This mob of petty nationalists and crosseyed gunmen was, again, reinforced by agents of Stalin. The I.R.A. was in clover ... I mean, that its members had resources such as passports, eighty per cent nitroglycerine dynamite, et cetera. So, these misguided fellows had a picnic planting time–bombs in railway cloakrooms, and so forth. Of course, they did little physical damage; killed a few women and children — but the *psychological* effect was important.

They alerted, and diverted, the Metropolitan Police and the City Police. Vigilance was redoubled all around the town. Now vigilance is a very good thing in a Police Force; it keeps it up to scratch, and that is all right. But double it, without an extra force of trained men, and you make for a nervous anxiety that cuts efficiency, and sends even disciplined officers jumping out of their skins to run, blowing whistles, in the direction of a car that has backfired.

Upon this I relied when, after the Irish outrages, I chose my time for stealing the Crown Jewels.

The Crown Jewels, as I have said, are guarded by something that works quicker than conscious thought: electricity. Ah, yes! — but even then, a million volts of lightning may be deflected by a copper spike, and run harmless into the ground through a copper ribbon.

A train of thought here, you see?

In 1939, the Tower of London got its electricity supply through cables that ran under Tower Hill ... Now, a calm and determined man who knew his timing could stop the power plants of the Boulder Dam itself, with a well-placed pocketful of gravel. By the same token, one properly-placed darning needle could put an end to the cerebration of an Einstein, a Schopenhauer, a Karmesin; in my case, once, temporarily, it was done with a mallet ...

To proceed: it occurred to me that if I could get at the cables that fed electricity to the Jewel Room in the Tower of London, all those protective electrical gadgets would be so much old iron, and all that marvelously intricate system of wires so much old rope. *Problem One:* How to cut the current? *Problem Two:* Having cut off the electricity, how to get at the Jewels?

The best means of approach to the Wakefield Tower, where the Jewels are kept, is by way of the River Thames. This is also the best place for a getaway, since there is always next to nobody on the river bank; while Tower Hill and Tower Bridge have their multitudes.

It was a stimulating little problem. The only thing about it, at that time, that made me uneasy was the fact that I should be compelled to employ assistance.

So I looked up an old friend of mine named Berry: one of those master craftsmen gone wrong that turn into burglars or forgers. He had been a metal-worker once upon a time; invented a new kind of oxyacetylene torch; got swindled out of the right, and fobbed off with a twenty-pound note. He declared war against society in his anger and frustration; took to making portable torches for safe-crackers; got involved, got three years. I saw to it that his children did not starve, and he was grateful for that.

Upon this one I knew I could rely. I told him what I wanted him to make and, by Heaven, he made it! It was a masterpiece — a ladder — but imagine a twenty-foot ladder, collapsible, so that you could hide it under your coat!

Berry made it out of some scrap metal from an old aeroplane. At the top of my ladder, I had fitted six hooks which were to have two functions: *One,* to hook the ladder to the Tower wall; *Two,* given the proper moment, to hook the Regalia through a hole which I proposed to burn in the steel and glass in the Jewel Room after I had cut off the current that protected it.

Berry made that oxyacetylene torch with the meticulosity of a jeweler. In its way, it was a kind of gem: the whole apparatus fitted into a gas-mask case, such as air–raid wardens were carrying at that time. Although Mr. Chamberlain had categorically stated that there would be no war, nevertheless wiser men so ordained it that the town was full of Air–Raid Precaution Officers, in appropriate uniforms ... Begin to get the idea?

There is no disguise as effective as a uniform, because if you are wearing a uniform — any uniform — nine hundred and ninety-nine people out of a thousand will look at it and not at you. Ask yourself that question: would you recognize your postman, your policeman, your milkman, if you met him on the street in plain clothes? Your grocer, even, without his apron? No. If you wish to be unrecognizable, look familiar. And, curiously enough, if you desire to be quite invisible, talk authoritatively in a raucous voice — their ears will blind them.

So. I had made three A.R.P. Wardens' uniforms. The plot thickens, you observe; what? Then, it was necessary to make contact with certain amenable fellows in the Tower Guard. They were Irish boys, of course, nurtured on legends about the I.R.A. Do not imagine that I imply that the Irish are a disaffected or disloyal people; they are very loyal, indeed — to the myths and legends of their race.

I found, partly by luck, two boys who were to be on guard at two points close to the Regalia Room, and represented myself as the fabulous Commandment Pat M'Hoginey who took the Rotunda in Dublin. I cannot speak Irish, but a very strong American accent with a certain inflection was convincing enough — with a bulge under my left armpit. These boys were incorruptible — they fell in with my scheme, waving aside all offers of reward. For the honour of Ireland, and the I.R.A., I could have the Crown Jewels; only, please, could I give them back Ulster?

We parted good friends, solomonizing in Mullaly's Wine Lodge ... What? You do not know what it is to solomonize? For a writer, you are not very strong on general knowledge. Many Irish distillers put out little bottles of whisky called 'babies'. One 'baby' is a heavy drink, so you divide it in two with a friend — splitting the 'baby', as in the Judgement of Solomon. We solomonized; and that was another part of the task accomplished.

Next, it was necessary for me to find out precisely where the electric cable traveled under the pavement to feed the Tower of London; and this I did by presenting myself to the Borough Surveyor as Mr. Cecedek, a Czech refugee prominent in textiles, looking for business premises and anxious to know about sources of electric power for his looms.

Now, I had to send one of my coadjustors to steal an electrical truck from another borough, which Berry repainted with the title, et cetera, of the local Borough Council of Stepney. Also, I had to purchase a rowing boat ... Surely, even you must have seen through my little scheme by now?

At the appointed time, Berry and one other would drive the truck to the vital cable plate, put up their workmen's screen, lift the plate, and wait — with synchronized watches — for the Zero Hour, as it is called, when they were to cut the main power cables.

Simultaneously, my other friend and I, in the uniforms of Air–Raid Wardens, would be rowing along the Thames towards the graceful lawn that separates the Tower of London from the river.

And, as I conceived and organized it, so it occurred. We arrived at the Tower, ran to the outer wall and climbed it by means of Berry's beautiful ladder ... See what I mean, now, when I say that mediocrity chooses an hour where genius picks its instant!

As I had arranged, precisely when we arrived at the Tower Wall, Berry and the other man cut the main power cable, and it was as if the Tower of London had shut its eyes. Everything went black; but I was prepared to find my way under that blanket of dark, you see.

We scaled the walls, reached the Wakefield Tower, rushed to the Regalia Room. My two sentries — here was where they came in — reporting 'All's well,' I cut through the steel and the glass, and, climbing into the broken cage, pulled out the Imperial State Crown and the King's Crown — which alone is set with the Koh–I–Noor diamond worth two million pounds. As for the Imperial State Crown, it is encrusted with 2,783 diamonds, 277 pearls, 18 sapphires, 11 emeralds, and 5 rubies.

Offhand, perhaps the most important haul I ever made.

And how did I get out? Exactly the way I came in. And how did I get away? Exactly as I had arrived. Because, you see, the River Police were not on patrol just then, and Scotland Yard had been alerted by me in connection with an I.R.A. plot to dynamite the House of Commons.

So I got away with those wonderful Crowns.

This took place Friday, the first of September, 1939. You know what happened on the Sunday morning: Great Britain declared war on Germany, and although I had an incalculable fortune in my hands and had, incidentally, fallen passionately in love with the Star of Africa, and the Black Prince's Ruby ... I don't know, there happened to my heart something difficult to put into words ...

I did not mind robbing a greasy millionaire; but even him I would not take from, if he were in trouble. How could I steal away something of the history of a valiant people going into battle? Again, I said to myself: "That nice King and his kind Lady have trouble enough without this."

So I nailed the Crowns up in a crate, and sent them to Scotland Yard. The affair — things being as they were — was hushed up. But the Tower of London, as you know, was closed for a time; and now, things being reorganized, it would take a better man even than I to steal so much as a spoon from the Jewel Room ...

... Karmesin sighed. I asked him: "What happened to 'King' Tombola?"

With infinite scorn, Karmesin said: "What, him? I intended to make him a nice little ersatz Imperial Crown, only he died through eating too much beef with red pepper. Goodnight."

Karmesin and the Royalties

"I wonder," I said to Karmesin, "why you don't write your life-story."

Karmesin let loose one of his elephantine laughs: *Heeeeeeaaaagh!* and slapped me on the back.

"I don't see what there is to laugh at in that?"

Karmesin, still laughing, replied: "But I do. No, my young friend, I cannot write my life-story. At least, I could write it. But I could never sell it."

"Of course you could."

"Not so, my enthusiastic young friend, not so. I have already sold it."

"To whom?" I asked.

"That is in itself a story," said Karmesin. He unraveled a little heap of cigarette-ends, and began to re-roll them. "I am one of the few people who has made nearly a hundred thousand out of an autobiography."

"A hundred thousand pounds!"

"Certainly. I have made money out of literature. Did you ever hear of my publishing venture? The opposite of *Who's Who*? I called it *Nobodies*."

"I never heard of it."

"Exactly."

"When was it published?"

"It never was."

"And when was your life-story published?"

"It never was."

"Then I don't see ..."

"My friend, you are a journalist, eh? Then I say to you: there is money in journalism; but more money is made out of works that never see the light."

"Will you explain all this?"

"Certainly," said Karmesin, poking out a tongue such as one usually sees on porcelain dishes in delicatessen shops, and moistening the gummed edge of a cigarette paper.

My Directory (said Karmesin) was my first venture in publishing. That was in America in 1914. I was living in a town with the barbarous name of Loco City. It had been a bad man's town in the eighteen-seventies, a silver town, where millions were made and lost in a day, and wild miners dashed down hatfuls of silver dollars in exchange for faked drinks. An eccentric millionaire of the type of Silver Dollar Yates had built the town on wild and rococo lines. There was an opera house, for example, with an auditorium large enough to contain three times the population of all Loco City; and a bar built to resemble the famous old Horse Shoe Bar in Chicago. It was so long that you were drunk on the smell of drink before you walked to the end of it.

But all that belonged to the past. In 1914, Loco City was populated by a new generation of townsmen; respectable middle-class American business men; estate-agents who called themselves Realtors; young men with rimless glasses who had forgotten how their grandfathers had loitered on the corners displaying notched gun-butts and Bowie knives.

It was all very simple. I started the Stars and Stripes Publishing Co., Inc., and began a local directory, which I called *Nobodies*. I drew up the histories of Loco City families. It read like the Newgate Calendar. Then I had a series of potted biographies of Loco City celebrities, and put down exactly what they did when they went to the capital cities on Buyers' Conventions ... how the President of the Loco City Bank had been seen carrying three intoxicated blondes in the streets of San Francisco; how another man, a buyer of mortgages, had been photographed wearing some lady's corsets, trying to milk a mule into a champagne-bottle in Memphis. It was very simple, I tell you, and very amusing. I sent galley-proofs of my Directory to the gentlemen concerned and they paid me not to put them in the Directory. Then I started a Social Register, and the same people paid me again to appear in its aristocratic columns; and then I left town with no less than fifty thousand dollars in my pocket. I could have made similar sums in every city of the United States, only I got tired of the business. I had a good idea for a variation of the Directory of the Directors — an exclusive little volume called *Is Their Credit Good?* — a list of business failures, settlers, and bankrupts. It is all very easy, as long as you don't cast aspersions on womanhood.

But this is only to illustrate how money can be made out of literature. I was speaking of my life-story. That is something quite different.

It was my last *coup*. When I think of it, I am sad, my friend. It was Karmesin's Hundred Days; the last flicker of the greatest brain in crime ... or out of it. What a man I was, then! What a brain was mine! I was like *Napoleon*.

So. In those days, I used to know a publisher, a very good fellow who is now dead. He was something of a wild man. I helped him out of a scrape — something to do with a woman with red hair who used to wait for him in his own waiting-room, with a loaded revolver in her left hand and a small bundle of incriminating letters. It was very nice. But it was he who said to me:

"My dear Karmesin, if you wrote your life-story, you would make money out of it."

"How much?" I asked.

"Well ... you might make a thousand pounds," he said, "or two thousand or even five ..."

He did not know what manner of man I was, this unhappy publisher, that he affronted me by even mentioning such disgusting small change, such birdseed to me! But I simply smiled and said:

"You assume that I should write a book for five — or may be only *one* — thousand pounds?"

"One might commission it," he said.

"And what, exactly, do you mean by that?"

"It is the practice of most reputable publishers," he said, "to advance money before a book is written, if they have confidence in the author."

"Oh," I said, and took him to lunch. I bought him three pounds-worth of food and drink, which took a bit of consuming at pre-war prices, and filled his mouth with a cigar as thick as your thigh. Have you got a cigarette? What was money to me, anyway? Easy come, easy go. Bah! Then I went away and thought.

I said to myself: "Just for fun, I will write a synopsis of my life-story, which I shall entitle: *I Have Stolen Five Millions*."

And I sat down, with a pad of cream-laid paper before me, and a pen with a wide nib.

I wish you could have seen that synopsis. It was great. Beginning with my early childhood, it covered about fifty years of my life. There was a crime on nearly every page. When there was not a crime, there was a criminal idea. I explained every unsolved crime-mystery since the year 1890, when I really got going in the business. Most of what I said was true. The affair of Lombard's Bank, the silly business of the gas meter, the affair of the Schnitzelbank Bonds, the horrible story of how I nearly became involved in the Xarro Valley Massacre, how I stole the Crown Jewels of the Maharajah of Bhang by means of a pot of glue and three pennyworth of tape, what happened to the famous Tyrone Opals, how I smuggled the Guayacum Pearls into Paris by means of an artificial hump, how I sent a message and a diagram to an agent of mine through three countries in every one of which a regiment of police were on the lookout, the reason why Goltensnobf the jelly-king has a nervous *tic* in his right eye, what happened to the Fourth Consignment of Opium — I tell you, a million things!

When I had finished, I found myself reading the thing with the liveliest interest. That is how good it was! I had succeeded in attracting my own attention, so that I put my synopsis down with a sigh, and thought: "What a man this Karmesin is, what a devil of a man!"

I tell you, there is no vanity like the vanity of authors. I was piqued. My curiosity was aroused. I wanted to see exactly how the publishing world would receive the synopsis that I had liked so much.

I went to a good typewriting agency, and I had about a thousand copies made, which I sent to every general publisher in England, Germany, America, and France. All the civilized countries.

Then I waited to see who would offer me most.

My first reply was from Kiljoy and Mudd, of Holborn. I had expected hysteria, wild compliments. They said something like this:

> Dear Sir,
> We have read your synopsis ... (and so on, and so on) ... which we find very entertaining.

Karmesin and the Royalties

> Although we are not in the habit of commissioning works of this sort, we might be prepared to make an exception in your case ...

and they went on, the imbeciles, to offer my something like £50 down, £25 on the day of publication, and twopence a week for life — some ridiculous nonsense. A royalty–basis of .025 per cent, on the first 500,000 copies — God knows. I don't remember. It was very little.

I roared with rage, and seized my heaviest walking–stick. Then I stopped, and laughed. It was too funny. Me! Karmesin! The greatest of all criminals, and the most successful, to be offered £75 for the inside story of his prodigious life! I laughed at the top of my voice, and put the letter in a drawer.

Soon, more letters came. One offered me £10 down for the world copyright. Another went so far as to suggest £100 down. They poured in. I got 700 replies, but the average of the offers was £50 I sent each one a letter saying: "Double your offer and I accept." Seeing what they would do.

No good. They wouldn't. I circularized the rest of the publishing business with my synopsis. You know I am a linguist. I got another hundred offers, in all kinds of dirty little sums in kronen, dollars, gulden, crowns, piastres, scudi, God only knows what Noah's Ark of currency.

And then, do you know what?

I found that I had wasted six months in this infernal literary work! Six months! It is true, I was not hard pressed for money, and was merely amusing myself seeing what they would do.

I awoke to the fact, however, that I was not properly appreciated. I was disgusted with the literary world. They were not my type. No. Besides, what should I write my story for? Pfui! Am I a society beauty? The devil I am! Bah. I said to myself: "My lad, you will write nothing more — ever!"

And I did not.

Karmesin furtively ate a piece of sugar. I said to him: "But all this leads nowhere. You said you made money out of your life–story. And now you say you abandoned the whole thing. What is one to believe?"

With terrible dignity, Karmesin looked down at me and said:

"Permit me, please, to finish what I was saying. I said that I would write nothing more. *Bon.* I also said to myself: 'You shall be revenged, my friend, on these book-men who treat you like an ordinary human being.' So I took my thick-nibbed pen, and wrote seven or eight hundred letters accepting every offer that was made to me, and, to cut a long story short, received about £40,000 from the whole of the world's publishing business, for the option on my life story."

"Which you never wrote, eh?"

"Quite."

"Hum," I said.

"And what the devil do you mean by 'Hum,' may I ask?"

"It doesn't sound probable."

"So. So—o. I am a liar."

"No, Karmesin, I didn't say that ... Besides, you said, at first, that you made £10,000. And then you said £40,000. Now what is one to think?"

"My young friend," said Karmesin, as one who reasons with a very small child, "am I to remember every trifling sum of money I have made and spent? Am I a clerk? Am I a book-keeper? Do I make the double-entry in seven different kinds of ink every time I buy a pair of bootlaces? 40,000, 50,000, 90,000, a 100,000 — bah, bah, bah, and bah! It is all birdseed, pocket-money. What can you do with £100,000? Are you a millionaire with such a sum? No. Then what is the use of it? *Ptcha.* In my room there are six empty beer-bottles. If you take them back to the off-license, we can get fourpence on each of them and get a packet of ten cigarettes. Let us go."

Skate's Eyeball

It was a notable criminal indeed that caused Karmesin to raise an eyebrow or twitch his moustache. Thus, when I said that a man called Carfax had never been caught, there occurred a certain convulsion in the features of Karmesin.

First, his eyebrows went up and his moustache came down, then his eyebrows leveled themselves and his moustache spread itself; he laughed. When Karmesin laughed, it was a sort of internecine incident — everything shook, yet he made little sound.

"Poor Carfax!" said Karmesin.

"Not so poor," I said. "Carfax got away with millions. Scotland Yard knows all about it — he fenced, fiddled, and organized. He rides about in an enormous limousine. Admit, Karmesin, that he must have made a couple of millions, and was never caught —"

"Never *what?* Never prosecuted, you mean," said Karmesin. "Neither was I. But *caught*, in the colloquial sense of the term? There I beg to differ."

Locking his enormous hands and glaring at me under his portentous eyebrows, making full play of his plum–like eyes, Karmesin went on, "Carfax's liquid assets were £2,530,700 in bullion, American dollars, and Swiss francs — I happen to know. But his fortune is gone, and his prestige is gone, and worst of all, he has lost face in his filthy mileu.

"Once upon a time, anyone who took a shilling off Carfax would be found at ebbtide in the Thames in the region of Greenwich, in an advanced state of decomposition. Now, he could not even get your arm broken. Well, I took a fortune off him as easily as — at least with less outcry than one might take a lollipop from a child. I'll tell you."

It was the autumn of the year 1945 that my peregrinations took me to a certain London hotel not far from Hyde Park which was a most peculiar hangout of black marketers, visiting film stars, and all that. In wartime your black marketers had tended to load and overload, now they felt certain misgivings. In the underworld it was a bull market today and a bear market tomorrow — an awkward time for a hard-working petty criminal or spiv to be operating.

To proceed: I was in the hotel bar, thinking my own thoughts and drinking a little glass of sound brandy, when there came to my nostrils — which are sensitive at the best of times — an unmistakable odour which I challenge the parfumiers of the world to reduplicate: the odour of a skate's eyeball.

In case you want to try it, put a pickled onion in neat Hollands gin and beer, and rinse and swallow. This, on the breath of a man who is afraid of dentists: work it out.

I lit a cigar and, without turning my head, said, "Carfax! Sit down. Stop breathing down my neck or I'll be compelled to go upstairs for a bath and a clean collar."

So Carfax sat down and offered a drink, but when I said that this was my table, and would he please order what he wanted — as if I did not know — he called for a wineglassful of Hollands gin, and produced from one of his pockets a little jar of pickled onions.

I said to him, "If you have anything to say to me, Carfax, turn your chair sideways and say it out of the other corner of your mouth." He did nothing of the sort.

Instead, he made me a kind of stream of consciousness, which ran somewhat as follows, "Karmesin, you're the one man in the world I'd cut my right hand off to see. My left, also. Karmesin, I know the boys, I've known 'em since Eddie Guerin escaped from Dartmoor, but never no one I could trust. Of all the tealeafs I've ever met, only you can work alone —"

Tealeaf, I need scarcely tell you, my young friend, is cant for thief. Try as he might, this fellow Carfax could not refrain from being offensive; everybody knows that I disapprove of slang.

However, keeping a smokescreen between myself and his skate's eyeball, I said nothing while Carfax went on, "Yes. There's the trouble with the wide boys — they got to have a pal. And believe me, Karmesin, it's been the downfall of too many. But sometimes a feller gets in a sort of jam; and it's then he needs a pal — for a consideration, mind you, for a consideration ...

"Now look at me; I'm the boss, I'm like a king, but who can I trust? For the little jobs, sure, I got a decent bunch of boys. They'd swing for anybody I put the finger on, and never squeal! Much good it'd do them if they did, because the world is a little place, and — get what I mean — they wouldn't die of old age. You can trust a bloke with your life, you can trust a bloke with your wife, but where will you find a bloke that you can trust with your money?

"Believe me, a gentleman is bloody hard to find. I don't mean somebody that talks with his mouth full of hot potatoes like you, because they're two a penny — what I mean is, one o' *Nature's* gentlemen, like me!"

"Perhaps," I said, "you think that it pays some dividends to put my legs under the same table with you? Listen, Carfax, I know that you can whistle up a mad–doggery of slashers; but I have not been afraid of the most desperate scum on earth from here to Marseilles, from Marseilles to Bucharest, from Bucharest to Hong Kong, and so on around the world.

"If threatened men live long, Mr. Carfax, I am assured of several hundred years of life." But he did not hear me.

He went on, "These Mayfair boys think they're gentlemen because they get their suits made in Savile Row. La–de–da! My boys, I outfitted 'em during the war by a tailor in Black Lion Yard; *he* made 'em a secret lining, and every one of 'em could carry clothing coupons, food coupons, and what not — and every one of 'em was dressed smart. To a point you can trust a man — say 20,000 coupons at a couple of shillings apiece; deduct overheads, and it's only a matter of a few hundred pounds. Yes? All right.

"What are you looking at me like that for? What did I do wrong? You're an educated man — What's Economics? Taking advantage of a necessity, I believe; in other words, filling up a hole, that's Economics.

"You're a man of education, so I don't need to tell you the meaning of bureaucracy. I'm a victim of bureaucracy. I had an Organisation tight as a drum and a mob clean as a whistle, that's agreed. Comes something ten times tighter, calling cop — that's bureaucracy for you.

"It comes around to this, Karmesin, you daren't let anybody know what you got, because once you let him know you trust him with it.

"Now I've got as lovely a bunch of boys as you could meet within spitting distance on a dusty day; but I pay 'em by the job, and provide bail when necessary. Karmesin, they love me like a father.

"I taught 'em all they know. They are as ignorant as dirt. Play both ends against the middle is Carfax's lay.

"Every one of 'em watches the other like a cat watches a mouse. Get me?"

I said, "Yes, my friend. But where do you get off?"

Carfax said then, "Where do I get off? Why, I'll be frank with you — just about here. Now there's only two boys I can trust — my sons. If anything happens to me they inherit through their mother."

I said, "Be more specific, Carfax."

His voice was hoarse as he explained. "Look. I'll tell you because it's no secret, but since 1939 I stacked up a pile of the dosh, only I daren't bank it and I daren't invest it. For why? Why, the police of two continents couldn't put salt on *my* tail, but there's one outfit that'll wait day and night and never let anything blow over.

"Know what I mean?"

I said, "That would be the Department of Inland Revenue."

Carfax said, "Listen, Karmesin, I'm getting on in years, and in the middle of the night I get a feeling like something's pressing exactly where you give a man the boot —" he pointed to his solar plexus — "so the little bit I saved up, the actuaries are after. They're scratching, Karmesin, they're digging.

"You know I switched trucks and lifted half a million pounds in Bank of England bullion from the airport; shipped it to France and had it cast into genuine coins, which I shipped back.

"The overheads were something terrible, but *that* I got away with. Murder I can get away with — put it like this, dead men tell no tales. Ah, you can hide anything you like," he said, "except money.

"I daresay I could be hanged many times over and the police know it, but they can't make a case against me. I've been grilled off and on for the past forty years by the cops, in the days when they were free with their hands too, but I never came across anything so dastardly cruel as the actuaries.

"Kind of put yourself in my position. I've got a little bit o' property. Put yourself in my position."

Knowing with whom I was dealing, I said, "Before I offer an opinion, Mr. Carfax, I will thank you for a consultant's fee — one hundred pounds, in one-pound notes."

As I expected, he said, "I could run to twenty-five pounds."

Whereupon, to his infinite astonishment, I replied, "Very well, Carfax, very well."

Having put the money in my pocket, I summed up. "Carfax, that you are a most notorious and sickening son of a dog is common knowledge in heaven and on earth. If you think you fool me for one instant, you never made a greater mistake in your misspent life.

"You do not need to tell me the circumstances; I will tell you. I know you to be a fence of thirty or forty years standing, and one of the ringleaders of the Black Market. But, friend Carfax, you were an exceedingly rich man long before the war brought the Yanks here. Only you were always a bully and a pig."

"Hold hard there, Karmesin! We've all got to fiddle a little. I mean to say, if I hadn't somebody else would've."

"I believe, Carfax, that I can foresee your every intention. What do you take me for? The little boy you pushed through the fanlight of a bank window and rewarded with a few pieces of silver?"

"The kid done it of his own free will," said Carfax.

"After you had shown him a razor. Sir, I am no such child. As I calculate, you must have accumulated — you were always a mean creature — something in the region of three million pounds. Now hear me out, Carfax.

"The most terrifying and incorruptible body of men is closing in on you. Never mind Scotland Yard; never mind M.I.5; never mind the F.B.I. and Interpol. Commend me, brother, to the Department of Inland Revenue, your bugbear. If you declare your earnings, or gains, about 99 per cent of the total will be forfeited. You are watched, and what you have you dare not spend. What you want is that I clear the way for you. Is that so?"

"You exaggerate the sum, you know," said Carfax. "But it's true the Inland Revenue has got narks and informers everywhere, so I daren't spend it — or keep it because that won't suit."

I continued, "I will proceed, having taken your twenty-five pounds. I was not born yesterday. All you can do with your miserable money is bury it in a hole in the ground; but while you might be content with that, your wife would certainly not. In fine, you want an outlet for your money."

"Well, all right."

"What outlet?" I asked. "Where an outlet? Carfax, it is my business also, to know what goes on in the world. Your only outlet is the United States of America. Your capital is in mixed currency, jewelry, and bullion —"

"Is it?" said Carfax.

I replied, "Now look here, Carfax, and I will give you the general line. Point One: 'good as gold' used to be a notable phrase in England, but gold in England is no longer good. Brother, you wouldn't get three jumps away with your bullion.

"Point Two: speaking of well-known jewelry, you have Lady Elphick's diamonds, worth on the open market a matter of two hundred thousand pounds.

"Three: you played the race-course with Straight-as-a-gun Ziggy, and came out with a fat profit. It's all right, Carfax, I know you paid Ziggy two thousand five hundred pounds for 'fixing.' Good enough?

"To proceed: you've got foreign currency which is more than your liberty is worth to push in the market. No, sir, you've got to get that load to France, and then to the United States. Contradict me if you dare!"

Carfax said, "Well, I wouldn't mind getting the stuff across the Channel and making a deal in France, if you get what I mean. What I mean to say, I can change it into something no bigger than four volumes of the works of Charles Dickens. These I can get to America, and the contents I know where to flog there. Do you foller me?"

I knew perfectly well, of course, what he would exchange his little fortune for. Obviously, heroin, cocaine, and morphine. So I said, "H, C, and M?"

"A word to the wise is sufficient," said Carfax. "Do you want to deliver?"

"On a percentage basis, naturally," I said.

"And what would you call a percentage basis?" he asked.

I said, "My dear Carfax, I am a man of business. First of all, there is a fee for transportation, in which I include certain actuarial risks. You must assume, Carfax, that my income is not low. You must also assume that if anything goes wrong, I am liable as an accessory to about ten years in prison.

"I am afraid that I must insist upon twenty thousand pounds in advance since you are carrying about three million; otherwise, no deal."

He said, "Karmesin, you're off your rocker. Call it ten thousand and we'll discuss."

"Go to the devil," said I.

We settled for fifteen thousand pounds.

But, fool though Carfax was, he knew how to make a bargain. He said, "How do we get the stuff over? And how do I get back? Little boat?"

"Plane," I said, "I have a good clean transport. I can drop you within twenty miles of Paris; put you in a car, bag and baggage, but — this is an important matter — you must tell me how long you are likely to keep me waiting."

"A matter of four hours. But where's your plane?"

"Between Bedford and Northampton. Private airfield," I said. "You will come with me by train, Carfax. If I guess rightly, one or two of your young men will be following by car — or your Sons, perhaps?"

Carfax said, "The trouble is, every dirty yobbo thinks he's an executive — you can't spit on a foggy night without hitting one. Believe me, I know. Like I said, there's only two boys in the world — apart from yourself — that I trust, and they are my Sons. And oh dear me, they don't trust each other.

"Who's the pilot?"

Now my pilot was a discreet fellow, an ex–night fighter who had made himself a marriage, got himself a little boy, and was trying to get a job doing stunts for the movies. His name was Flight Lieutenant Canless.

He could not get a position in civil aviation because of honourable injuries.

However, I said, "Carfax, the least said the better. We have all fallen into the soup in our time. In any case, I'll stand by."

He said, "I'll bet you will. But come on now, fair play, eh? You'll stand by me, but a couple of my boys will stand by you, Karmesin. I ought to warn you that I arm 'em with —"

"Save your breath which, I may say, is redolent. You arm your boys with .25 automatics loaded with steel–jacketed bullets; they make little noise, but have penetrative power.

"Carfax, there is nothing at all you can tell me that I do not already know."

Carfax said grudgingly, "This I know. But you get your pay only when I'm safe back in England."

I said, "With your little parcels? Very well, Carfax — not that I approve of what the French call stupéfiants, and the English call narcotics."

He said, "Supply and demand. What more do you want?"

"Nothing more," I said, "nothing. Three days from now I will pick you up at Euston in time for the seven o'clock train. I have not the slightest doubt that a couple of your young men will be following in a souped-up Cadillac."

"How did you know it was a Cadillac?"

Disdaining to reply, I said, "Seven o'clock Thursday evening at Euston station, Carfax, and you have my word on it that you shall be delivered safe on English soil, with nothing to embarrass you."

"I'd better be, you know."

"Meet me, then, and we take off from my private airport."

Carfax said, "I've got to have a hand with me, Karmesin, because — not to lie to you — I'm carrying weight, and I've got a bit of the old blood pressure. The buzzing, if you get what I mean, between the ears and up the back of the neck."

I said, "Enough, Thursday."

"Ah, but you don't get a penny, you know, until I'm safe back."

I said, "This has already been discussed. Good evening."

So Carfax went his way and I went mine, and as I walked — always with an object in view — I argued with myself as follows. Take this creature. He is almost too clever to live. Who is the greatest fool in the world? Why, the cleverest, because he grows to be the most vain.

Then I went to one of those funfairs, one of those places where people flirt with death. I say "flirt" advisedly, because there is no intention of a consummation. They have not the slightest fear in the anticipation; for they know there will be no consummation. The same thing happens in lovemaking, with which I am not concerned this past forty years. There are women who, as the saying goes, tease.

By the same token, there are people who love to tease the old man with the scythe. Thus, the apparently dangerous fun and games — your roller–coasters, and what not — are vastly popular in places of amusement. By the same token, immense popularity attaches to games where you throw things, fire small arms, and so on.

Now in a funfair to which I went there was young Flight Lieutenant Canless who owned a concession. He had been in trouble in his time, and I had helped his mother a little bit. A pound here, a pound there — what's the difference? The boy Canless got into bad company. He got into quite good company a few years later when he became a night fighter in the Battle of Britain.

Young Canless was one of those boys with a peculiar knack for machinery combined with a sense of quiet desperation. The two go together. Fearing everything, he set his teeth and feared nothing.

He was shot down somewhere and lost an arm. The war being over, I advised him that now was the time for gaiety.

In point of fact, I helped to purchase an old transport plane which, on the ground, could go through all the gyrations of a night fighter: sixpence for two minutes. It was a valuable attraction.

So I went to where Canless was, and said to him that I wanted a favour, for which I'd be prepared to pay.

He said to me, "I owe you plenty favours, Mr. Karmesin. Don't talk about pay. Name the favour."

Pointing to his machine, I said, "This contraption: it can loop the loop, roll, dip, drop, and all that?"

"All that, and tailspin too."

"Is it transportable, Canless?

"Oh yes. I hitch her to a tractor. She can't fly, you know, but I can cover the country with the old cow."

I then said, "I don't know what you make a day around here. But I will guarantee you one thousand pounds for twenty–four hours of your time and the use of this lump of ironmongery. Do you happen to have a strong and resolute friend?"

"There's Cheerful Charlie, who helps around the lot. He was my favourite erk. Bit shortsighted, and weighs fourteen stone. Was nearly heavyweight champion of the Air Force, only — you know how it is — man couldn't keep his chin down. Stuck his face forward and his neck out. We used to call him the turtle. But game as a pheasant, and will fight like a stag; and what with the hidings he's taken, his face is something to haunt your dreams. But what's the gen? Is it legit?"

"It is not merely legitimate," I said, "it is humanitarian.

"Bring your machinery and Cheerful Charlie to Nobbutt in Northamptonshire. It is a flat piece of country, distinguished only by the fact that the demented poet William Cowper and his pet hare lived nearby. It is also not far from Bedford which, as you know, gave out a slightly deranged tinker named John Bunyan who wrote *The Pilgrim's Progress*.

"Arriving at Nobbutt, inquire for Karmesin's field. There, set up this piece of nonsense, you and your turtle, and wait for me. You will find it best to set up shop close by a prefabricated hut or waiting-room, which I'll provide.

"It is also my intention that you and your turtle carry arms — unloaded. These I have: one, a U.S. Army .45 automatic; the other, an English revolver of the same calibre. Loaded or unloaded, anything one aims at with these things is quite safe. Now here is five hundred pounds, and I rely on you."

Canless did not want to take the money, but he took it and agreed to be with Charlie and his apparatus at the appointed spot somewhat in advance of the appointed time. There was to be discreet lighting — very discreet.

He introduced me to Charlie the erk, and I could not have wished for a better man. He had a military bearing — but it was at an angle of about thirty degrees — and his ears were thickened; put yourself in a crate with that man, and you might come out badly; only he was wearing a pair of Army issue steelrimmed glasses, even with which he had to get within two feet of an object before he could discern it.

I said to Canless, "You will be pilot, of course. Let this one be air hostess, or steward. Buy him a white jacket, a blue cap. I leave it to you."

So I went back to Carfax and told him to get set. In his usual manner, he said, "Karmesin, old cock, in this mob we generally use a .25 automatic with steel-jacket bullets. But you're a big fellow, so I'm packing a 9 mm Luger."

I replied, "I never carry arms. But if you frighten me to death you will lose your means of transportation. In short, tell it to the Marines and be ready for the train."

He was worried, and said, "Dog doesn't eat dog."

"There are dogs and dogs," I said.

So we made our arrangements, to cut a long story short, and got on the train.

Please allow me a little philosophy. It is not much I ask of life — a little philosophy, a little psychology. With, perhaps, a shot of metaphysics, and a dash of bitters one acquires? I say that this Carfax, the most astute criminal in England, was easier to rob than a baby.

To cut it fine, I used a child's trick on this over-subtle fellow. We got out to the airfield, if I may so call it, where I had set up that aeroplane.

Rest assured that Carfax was at my elbow, and his goons — as I think they call them — not far behind. They carried the bullion to the extent of about, in troy weight, seven hundred pounds.

Flight Lieutenant Canless was at the controls in a blue cap, and an electric sign went on saying:

NO SMOKING
PLEASE FASTEN YOUR SAFETY BELT

The doors were slammed, the engines turned over, and then the fun began.

I suppose you know that you can take about three minutes of one of these toy aeroplanes. Try it, I suggest, for two and a half hours — this piece of engineering performing every known gyration to the thirty-two points of the compass.

I was there for psychological effect. From time to time I shouted, "It looks like we are going into the drink!" — at which signal Canless would do a nosedive, a tailspin, and a sort of bellyroll. The plight of Carfax and Co. was something pitiful to see.

From time to time I bellowed warnings about being in the drink, and all that. Carfax, crushed, begged for mercy after a couple of hours.

At a signal from me, we looped the loop a couple of times, bumped in the most sickening manner, then steadied ourselves. Eventually, bump-bump-bump, we landed.

Only, you see, we had never left the ground — in that time a few of those surrealist French travel posters had been put in my little hut. A few artistic touches, a bottle of Armagnac, a copy of *Le Rire*, et cetera.

I have never seen a sorrier handful of criminals than Carfax and his boys when they got out of what used to be a plane. I said, "Powerful car here. Put the bullion in the boot." So, very unsteadily, they did.

Then I said, "Now, Carfax, I'll trouble you for that canvas belt round your waist."

I added, "For goodness sake, don't try to pull one of your little guns, because my friends and I carry things of larger calibre. Furthermore, you could not hit the side of a barn at ten feet, so be sensible.

"Unbuckle, Carfax, and if you pull out the wrong thing, one of us will let you have it in the stomach — which, I believe, is sufficiently empty after your little trip to contain a few grammes of lead. Your boyfriends, also, are moving in circles, while we are steady as stones.

"Will you have the goodness to unbuckle your belt? Or shall one of my friends be your valet de chambre?"

Carfax said, "Karmesin, I'll get you for this!" But he let fall a canvas belt about twelve inches wide.

Canless picked it up and handed it to me. I had to drape it about my shoulders, Carfax was such a big man.

Suddenly, he whimpered, quite demoralised, "How do we get back to England?"

"You have your passports and some money in your pockets," I said. "Everything else failing, go to the Consulate and weep. Now, if you take the road straight ahead, bear left, hit the main road for about eight miles, you will find yourself at a perfectly respectable railway station."

"You promised —"

"I promised to land you on British soil," I said, "and so I have. You are equidistant between Bedford and Northampton. Charlie, hitch the tractor to that contraption and take it back to the funfair.

"Canless, get at the wheel and let her roll!"

Carfax said; in a broken voice, "Karmesin, I'll split fifty–fifty."

I replied, "What kind of a fool do you take me for, when I have the whole lot?"

So, while Charlie drove the machine back to the funfair by means of a tractor, Canless drove me at high speed to London.

On the way I told him, "Apart from what you get, remember that there is a moral in this. A child could not have fallen for this lay, but that corrupt creature did. It was a child's trick — which leads me to conclude that, tough as they think they are, a child can lead them."

"Oh well," said Karmesin, "the proceeds, as I told you, amounted to £2,530,700 — we will ignore the odd shillings. Every penny of this I gave to the Rehabilitation Fund of Free Europe, deducting for myself only twenty per cent plus out-of-pocket expenses. For my work in this matter I charged nothing.

"And that is why your famous Carfax is now reduced to an endowment policy which, to him, is abject poverty. True, he owns the freehold of his home in Highgate — but he is reduced to the level of a petty rentier and, the cost of living being what it is, he is a poor man.

"Worst of all, as I told you, he dare not lift a finger now, even to get me knocked on the head."

Karmesin, if not the greatest criminal, at least the greatest and most plausible liar of his time, then added, "Carfax has no influence any more, even among those who used to worship him. And upon what did this worship depend? Upon the fact that Carfax was safe because he was rich. It is not for me to moralise, but riches and respect go together."

Grinding out a twice-rolled butt under the heel of a well-worn shoe, he said, "Do you happen to have a fresh cigarette about you?"

Oalámaóa

In any circumstances my friend Karmesin is rather better than life-size, but when the weather turns chilly and he puts on his winter overcoat, passers-by sometimes run around the block to see him again, advancing in all his outrageous majesty. For in this coat, which is of some moth-eaten blackish-gray fur, with his great red face and his moustache which, like the philosopher Nietzsche's, hangs down in corkscrew curls, he has the air of a hard-up Jove wrapped in his last leaky thundercloud.

"Oh, let people look," he said to me, "they will never see a coat like this again. It is the last."

"Too bad," I said.

"Yes. It is made of the fur of the Mongolian Syrax. This pelt was taken off an extinct beast found frozen along with the mammoths in the Siberian snows." He shot his cuffs. "You know, considering it is forty-seven thousand years old, it is not very much the worse for wear."

Now Karmesin has been described as either the greatest crook or the greatest liar the world has ever known. But how is it possible to reconcile the evident pennilessness of this remarkable man with his accounts of his unfailing success as a master thief? And, if you know Karmesin, you ask yourself, "How is it possible that such a man could condescend to lie?"

Mongolian Syrax, for example! There was no mention of any such beast, extinct or otherwise, in any available reference work. No furrier had ever heard of such a creature. Yet I still feel in my heart that somehow or other the authorities must be wrong. "Look at the Piltdown Skull," I say to myself. "Oh, surely, there must have been one — just *one* — Mongolian Syrax!"

Such is the power of the man.

He rolled himself a cigarette fat as a cheroot, and put it between his lips. Under that portentous moustache it looked no bigger than a thermometer.

He said, "I once made a little money out of a kind of overcoat. I cannot bother to recall the exact amount. Tens of thousands — there are people nowadays to whom it would be a small fortune, I hear. Offer me a cup of coffee and I will tell you about it."

In the café Karmesin settled himself comfortably, pocketed four lumps of sugar and some tooth picks, and went on:

The overcoats to which I refer (said Karmesin) were, in fact, coats of paint, and the cloth was second-hand canvas. Yes, they were pictures, supposed to be the work of the French artist Paul Gauguin. Even the likes of you, my friend, will have heard of Gauguin, since I am told both Mr. George Sanders and Sir Laurence Olivier portrayed him in *The Moon and Sixpence*.

As a character, Gauguin cannot miss with the general public: he deserted his family, swindled his friends, thrashed his mistresses, and (to paraphrase Mr. Longfellow) departing left behind him toothmarks in the hands that fed him.

But he painted some quite decorative pictures in the South Seas. They make suburban homes look artistic, especially in light oak frames. And although he was poor in his unsavory lifetime, some time after his death his pictures became immensely valuable. So, since his brushwork is not too difficult to imitate, the faking of Gauguins was, until recently, something like a little industry in itself.

For example, I knew an innkeeper near Arles who made twenty million francs by selling a Gauguin portrait of his grandfather, purported to have been left by the painter in lieu of cash for an unsettled bill. The innkeeper sold two hundred and eighty of these "originals" before he retired — used to buy them by the dozen from a dealer in Marseilles; nail one over a hole in the chicken coop, and wait for a tourist to "discover" it.

You see, even if your sucker can be persuaded that he has been caught, he can generally be relied on to keep his mouth shut. He loathes being revealed as a fool. That is why so few clever fakers of works of art are exposed in their lifetimes.

But by about 1945 mere copies of famous paintings by Paul Gauguin became a drug on the market. By that date, it has been calculated; more than five million dollars had been spent on spurious originals of one canvas alone, the one named *Te Po*. It was necessary to discover a hitherto unheard-of Gauguin picture.

I gave only a passing thought to the matter, being occupied with more lucrative affairs just then. But as luck would have it, I ran into an impecunious painter named Molosso — and here, if you like, was an extraordinary type! He was, in a way, a little like the Dutch hero, van Meegeren, who painted pictures alleged to be by old Dutch masters with such consummate skill, and such scientific meticulousness, that he fooled all the German experts, and got undisclosed millions out of such collectors as the Reichsmarshal Goering.

Van Meegeren reproduced the same pigments that the old masters had used, ground out of identical earths and jewels in the same kind of mortars with exactly similar pestles; and he applied his paint with hair-for-hair reconstructions of the old brushes, upon genuine but worthless contemporary canvases, copying the strokes of the great artists to the tiniest capillary, with an exquisite perfection of microscopic skill that has never been equaled.

Or perhaps it has? What van Meegeren did, might not someone else have done? Da Vinci's *Mona Lisa*, in the Louvre, is alleged by some experts to be a fake. Believe me, my young friend, some strange stories might come out if some of our famous art galleries were carefully examined today!

Well, my little Molosso was a lesser van Meegeren. I really marvel at this kind of man — I am lost in wonder, that one who can paint a new picture as superbly as, say, Vermeer would have painted it if he had chosen the subject, should not elect to be a great genius in his own right. Why didn't this titanic faker van Meegeren cry, "But *I* am the master!"

I can only assume that his genius was not strong enough; it had its rotten spot, and poverty found it, so that he argued, "Why should I go hungry as van Meegeren, when I can drink champagne by pretending to be Vermeer?" So he faked, and it was a great joke. But it was also a pitiful tragedy, an Allegory of Genius Strangled by Greed.

Little Molosso started to paint with a high spirit and a light heart. But your true artist must be made of tough stuff, and Molosso wanted heart. A great man can whitewash a barn for a bit of bread without losing the glory and the dream; but when Molosso learned that the world preferred to spend its money on greeting cards rather than canvases, he drifted into the position of a disgruntled mediocrity who enjoyed being what they call "misunderstood."

He would have gone to the dogs completely but for his wife, a cheerful little woman, who adored him and took his ill-treatment of her as matter of course. And in abusing her Molosso could feel as a hungry genius is romantically supposed to feel — that if he had been a man like Gauguin, with spirit enough to leave her abruptly with a parting punch in the jaw, he might have been recognized as great. As it was, he was kind enough to stay married to her and let her work for him.

For her sake I decided to make Molosso rich.

The idea came to me suddenly one evening after I had walked home with him from the printer's office at which, I being there on business, he had scraped an acquaintance with me. I was amused by his preposterous virulence — it broke out when we were passing a printseller's shop. Rembrandt painted with mud, he shouted, Da Vinci was a plumber, van Gogh painted in Braille for the blind, and as for Gauguin — *bah!* — he, Molosso, had painted better when he was eighteen!

"And if you don't believe me, come upstairs and I'll prove it," he said.

Having time to kill, I went to see what he had to show. And indeed, Molosso really did have a most peculiar talent. Alas, it was a talent without soul! He was so empty of original spirit that he almost frightened me.

How shall I put it? If you asked him to depict, for instance, a landscape he had seen, he would stand helpless, paralyzed, while the paint dried on his palette. But if you said, "Molosso, paint me a landscape as Salvator Rosa, or Turner, or Van Gogh *might* have painted it," why, then he would go to work at once, with tremendous energy, and the results would have been astonishing — if he had not tired of the game in the middle.

Since we had been talking of Gauguin, he pulled out a half-finished canvas, saying, "There. Painted when I was eighteen. I'd thought of passing it off as genuine to some fat pig of a collector, just to show my disdain for collectors in general, and that leprous charlatan of a Gauguin in particular. But I thought, oh, what the devil, they are beneath my contempt! But look — there's your precious Gauguin in every stroke, every line, every vulgar splash of eye-catching color. It was to have been a variation on one of that ham-fisted stockbroker's Polynesian themes. I was going to call it *Oalámaóa*."

"Meaning?" I asked.

"Meaning simply *Oalámaóa* — men, pigs, women, hibiscus, and bananas. What else is there in the Pacific?"

I looked closely and long. And it was then that my scheme sprouted, swelled, and blossomed to perfection like one of those Japanese paper flowers in warm waters.

Now, as I was about to speak, Molosso's wife came in, carrying a package of groceries and three bottles of wine. He did not even say "Hello" to her — simply jerked a thumb in her direction and said to me, "That's Lucille, the cross I have to bear."

I said, "Madame, I am most impressed by your husband's work, and propose to offer him a commission worthy of his brush."

"What does she know?" cried Molosso. "She sews buttons on rich women's drawers in a lingerie shop in the Rue de Miromesnil. But are you serious, sir? A commission?"

"If you are free," I said.

"Free! I wish I were!" said Molosso, with a bitter look at his nice little wife. "But sir, I'd do anything in the world rather than continue to paint sickening cherubs and nauseating roses for Minard's Hand-Painted Greeting Cards."

"Work for me for six months, then," I said, "and I will pay you one thousand dollars American every month. All your expenses will be paid. At the end of our association, I will pay you thirty thousand dollars in cash. Well?"

Well! So began what must be the neatest piece of polite skullduggery that even the rare picture business has ever known. And these, my friend, are very strong words indeed.

So. A few months later I called on no less a person than Mr. Egon Mollock, in his suite at the Crillon. He had come to Paris for his usual annual visit, seeking what he might devour, for he was a multimillionaire and a collector. Of what? Of anything that nobody else had, of anything any other collector would give his ears for.

He was not a lover of beauty; only of rarity. If wart hogs had been scarce he would have collected wart hogs. As it was, he went after original works of art, which he kept locked up in his mansion in Connecticut.

To this loveless jailer of the beautiful, I said, "I have news for you, in confidence, Mr. Mollock. Imogene Grible wants to sell a Gauguin."

"Very likely," said he. "But I happen to know that the Gobseck Collection is entailed."

"Exactly. That is why I am empowered to speak to you — in the strictest confidence."

I should explain, here, that Lucian Gobseck was one of those mystery men of money whose histories always have to be hushed up. He came up overnight like a toad stool, and helped to finance Louis Napoleon's *coup d'état;* had a long, murky career as company promoter, moneylender, and unofficial pawnbroker to the great, and died in 1899, leaving a colossal fortune and an art collection which hardly anyone has ever been allowed to look at.

The collection is entailed — in other words, it is an heirloom; it may be inherited, but never sold. And such an inheritance, nowadays, is the legatee's nightmare. There is many a proud inheritor who, ruined by death taxes and insurance premiums, prays day and night for a good hot fire fanned by a hard dry wind.

Gobseck's only child, a girl, reversed the accepted order of things. Generally, it is an American heiress who marries a penniless Frenchman. She married a cowhand out of Buffalo Bill Cody's Wild West Show, named Boscobel, said to be the most optimistic poker player on earth.

But even so, their daughter Imogene brought a large fortune to her husband, a Bostonian named Gribble, who abhorred gambling and invested only in sure things at twelve-and-a-half per cent. Thus, when he passed on — Bostonians never die, they simply pass on — Imogene was left with only about $25,000 a year, and this incubus of a Gobseck Collection to keep up and pay insurance on.

I said, "The Tonkin Necklace has been broken up and replaced with a paste replica these five years. So has the Isabella Tiara. Morally, Imogene Gribble is justified; in law, she is culpable. I feel that I am no more a purveyor of stolen property in offering *Oalámaóa*, than you would be a receiver of it if you bought it. This kind of technically illicit deal is less reprehensible than, say, smuggling a bottle of cognac. Nobody is the loser, but everyone gains. A copy of *Oalámaóa* molders in the dark instead of the beautiful original; Mrs. Gribble has some money, which she needs; I draw my commission; and you have the joy of possession —"

"— *Oalámaóa*? I never heard of it," he said.

"Neither had I until I first saw it," I told him. "It is possible that old Gobseck foresaw Gauguin's value, and bought some unheard-of canvases. Who knows?"

"I have met Imogene Gribble," said Mollock, looking at me with that unpleasant smile of his, which has been so aptly likened to a tired earthworm trying to bite its other end. "What is to prevent my dealing with her directly?"

"If the lady chose to deal directly, I imagine she would not have employed me as a go-between," I said with some coldness. "Mrs. Gribble mentioned three of her acquaintances whom I might approach in this matter: Karyatidis the ship-owner, Gregor Dreidl the theatrical man, and your good self."

"Why did you come to me first — if you did come to me first?"

"Because," I said with a shrug, "Karyatidis is on his yacht, Dreidl is in New York, and you happen to be in Paris."

"Well," he said, grudgingly, "I'll look at the picture."

I had it with me. Mollock, who had done so much under-the-counter buying in his time, remarked on the fact that the canvas was still stretched in its framework. He had rather expected it to be rolled up in a cardboard tube.

I reminded him, "This is not a stolen canvas, my dear sir, cut from its framework with a razor blade. Why mar it even that little, therefore?"

"This is no Nineteenth Century canvas," he said.

"Of course not. It is very much older. The art dealer, Père Tanguy, from whom most Parisian artists of Gauguin's time got their supplies, had a considerable stock of perfectly good canvases painted by unheard-of mediocrities of every century. The pictures were worthless; the canvases were excellent. So impecunious painters often bought them for a few francs, cleaned them, and painted over them. This you must know. Ah ..." I said with a sigh, "... whoever sold Gauguin that bit of canvas is still whistling for his money, I'll wager, wherever he is!"

"But what a blaze of color!" he exclaimed.

So it was. There was something stunning in the impact of the color of *Oalámaóa* as it hit your eye. Little Molosso, in his vanity and his spite, had out-Gauguined Gauguin, so to speak.

The central figure was a golden-skinned woman, nude, walking as if under a spell, followed by a group of young men wearing lava-lavas of different tints but all marked with the same meandering tantalizing design. They were coming out of a jungle flaring with flowers. To the right, in the foreground, a black-and-white pig rooted among the shrubs.

I said, "He must have enjoyed himself, that man, painting this picture."

Mollock nodded. "I wonder what that pattern means, there on the cloth."

"Some Polynesian ideograph, no doubt," I said.

"And how much does Imogene Gribble want for this?" he asked.

"One hundred and fifty thousand dollars," I said.

"Like hell she does," said he. "Do you realize that if I don't buy, a word dropped by me will make the sale of this picture to anybody else absolutely impossible?"

"Sir," said I, "in naming you, Karyatidis, and Dreidl, Mrs. Imogene Gribble referred only to the three most respectable of her list of potential buyers."

I will not bore you with an account of the negotiations that followed. They started before lunch, and ended at cocktail-time. Mollock wheedled me. Mollock tempted me, and at last I fell. With an air of shame I accepted $105,000 as the "official" price paid for *Oalámaóa* in this highly unofficial deal, and an extra fifteen thousand dollars strictly off the record as my price for underselling my employer.

Mollock was very good at figures.

He put it to me, "Say I pay a hundred and thirty-five thousand for *Oalámaóa*. Your dealer's commission, twenty per cent, amounts to twenty-seven thousand dollars, and that is that. But say I pay only a hundred and five thousand, and give you a private honorarium of fifteen thousand, you make thirty six thousand and I save fifteen."

You can't argue with arithmetic. An expert having, after a secret examination of the picture, pronounced it "The Gauguin to end all Gaugins," I took my money and Mollock sailed for America. My little game was well begun.

... Yes, you heard me correctly — *begun*. Do you think a man like me expends such creative planning and precise administrative work for a wretched $120,000? Do you take me for a common crook?

To proceed: as soon as he got home, Mollock had his new acquisition suitably framed and lighted, and gave a select little dinner for a few of the collectors he hated most, and *Oalámaóa* was unveiled. The effect was all he had hoped it might be; Mollock savored to the full the joy of seeing the unfeigned admiration of his guests for the picture, and their ill-disguised envy and loathing for himself.

Dreidl, the theatrical man, offered him $180,000 for the picture, on the spot. This finagler had turned himself into something called a Fine Arts Development Corporation, among other slippery things, and could somehow elude the tax collectors in his artistic sidelines by pretending to be a dealer. But our Mr. Mollock would not sell. He wanted to gloat. *Oalámaóa* was his alone!

I let him wallow in his base triumph for several days. Then I sent one of my friends to Mollock in the guise of a visiting French expert. This reliable man, whom I had most thoroughly drilled in his role, looked at the picture, did what the theatrical people call a double-take, and burst out laughing.

"Why!" he cried. "Bless my soul, but what a clever little rascal Molosso turned out to be, after all! I never thought he had it in him to stick to one thing for so long, though."

"What are you talking about? And who is Molosso?"

"A painter of greeting cards for Minard, in Paris. You have probably seen his signature on the more expensive kinds of birthday felicitations, wedding congratulations, et cetera, et cetera. You may certainly see his highly noticeable signature — he is a vain little fellow — in all its glory on this excellent fake. Why, the rogue has had the consummate impudence to paint his name openly — but openly — all over it!"

And he pointed out that interesting meandering design on the men's draperies in the picture — the very design Mollock had been the first to point out, and which I had said might be some Polynesian ideograph.

"See, sir — you need no magnifying glass — this is simply Molosso's regular signature over and over again. See? *Molosso-molossomolosso*, with the loops filled in. But oh, what a beautiful joke!"

I need scarcely tell you that Mollock failed to see the beauty of it. But he was a hard man, and a ruthless man, and a quick-thinking and a persuasive man. He talked to my friend the "expert"; he wheedled him, he tempted him, and, like me, my friend fell. He agreed, for a consideration — $5000 down, and $5000 more on completion of the deal — to sell *Oalámaóa* to the Greek magnate Karyatidis.

First, Mollock let it be rumored that on account of some unfortunate speculations in Africa he might be compelled to sell part of his collection. It was not true, of course — the man was a born liar. And then Karyatidis was delicately approached in the matter of the *Oalámaóa*.

Mollock knew his brother art-graspers: if he owned a picture and Dreidl desired it, then Karyatidis would stop at nothing to get it. Then he wrote us an ambiguously worded authority to act for him in the sale of his recently acquired canvas, *Oalámaóa*. "Gauguin never painted better," he said in the note. But he did not say that Gauguin had painted *Oalámaóa*.

And Karyatidis bought the picture for $210,000, to hang in the saloon of his yacht. Of this not untidily round sum, I sent Mollock not one penny. And when he began to act in a generally offensive, resentful manner, I took little Molosso to see Karyatidis, and I said, "M. Karyatidis, you have nothing to fear from Mollock. His hands are tied and his lips are sealed. You have only to threaten him with criminal proceedings for trying to sell you a fake Gauguin."

"What fake Gauguin?"

I pointed out the cunning device of Molosso's signature. I presented Molosso, saying, "Here is the man who painted the picture entitled *Oaldmaóa*, which now adorns your saloon."

Karyatidis had not risen from fig-packer to multimillionaire by being easily surprised. He rubbed his chin, and looked me up and down, and said, "What's your angle? Make it good."

"Why," I said, "M. Molosso was employed to paint over the original Gauguin, so that the canvas might not fall into enemy hands during the war. The true *Oalámaóa* is underneath the one you see. M. Molosso will clean the canvas, and you will be the possessor of the original after all. Only Mollock will be out of pocket. I, sir, am the thief here, and nobody else."

"And what is the subject of the picture underneath?" asked Karyatidis.

"*Oalámaóa*," I said, "but without Molosso's signature on the draperies."

"All right," said Karyatidis. Then he went on to indicate, in a soothing voice, that if I double-crossed him I would soon wish I had never been born; the ocean beds, from Alexandretta to Caracas, were white with the bones of men who had tried to double-cross Karyatidis. It was not the money, he said, but the principle.

I told him point-blank that I had double-crossed better men than he when he was unhygienically boxing figs for his living in Istanbul.

"I know," he said. "You must have something up your sleeve, or why come to me at this point, when you could be far away with two hundred and ten thousand of my money? You must know you'll never get another penny out of me."

"Perhaps you will get a penny out of me," I said. "I mean, at the expense of someone you don't like."

"Ah, that! An enemy's penny brings good luck," he said. "I like you. I could use a man like you in my business."

"Compliment for compliment, I could use a man like you in mine," I told him.

Well, then Molosso went to work: off came *Oalámaóa*'s top coat, and there was a similar picture underneath; only, as I had said, the pattern of the embroidery was different, on the man's garments. Molosso's signature was gone.

"The difference is obvious, now," said Karyatidis.

"Isn't it?" I said. "And here is your enemy's penny." I gave him an envelope. "This," I told him, "contains a sheet of white paper bearing a perfect impression of Molosso's right thumb in ivory black. Look carefully at the lower right-hand corner of *Oalámaóa*, and you will see, deep in the original paint, an identical thumbprint."

"Are you telling me *this* is a fake, too?"

"Absolutely. But wait. You do not like Mr. Dreidl, I believe? Well, he will come to you and beg you to sell this *Oalámaóa*, and you will let him have it at a profit. And I will take dealer's commission."

With this, I left him; he was absolutely bewildered, perhaps for the first time in his life.

So I went to visit Gregor Dreidl in his indecently voluptuous office, and I told him, as one crook might tell another, of the whole affair, and he was tremendously amused. But he stopped laughing when I said, "The cream of the jest is, that underneath this second *Oalámaóa* — *There is a third!* And this one at the bottom is the genuine one!"

And after so much tedious palaver that to give you a mere précis of it would make me so hoarse that I should be compelled to ask you for more coffee, Dreidl went to Karyatidis and bought *Oalámaóa* for $225,000 and one cent. The Greek insisted on that penny; had to have it brand-new, too. Later, I heard, he had it mounted in diamonds and used it for a scarf pin.

I took my twenty per cent, and, having grown bored with the affair, concluded it in the following manner:

I went to Mollock, who, to put it mildly, upbraided me. That *Oalámaóa* he had paid good money for was a fake, he cried. I said yes, I knew, and I was much to blame; for the fake had been deliberately overpainted on the original. But this, I said, was not the worst of it. *Paul Gauguin himself had perpetrated a kind of fake!*

"I mean," I said, "that Gauguin was paid to disguise an immensely valuable old master with a comparatively worthless original of his own — oh, Mr. Mollock, Mr. Mollock — that *Oalámaóa* was painted over *The Stoning of St. Stephen*, by El Greco, and I would give my right arm to get it back!"

Dazed, he said, "Somebody painted a fake Gauguin over a real Gauguin, who painted over a genuine El Greco?"

"Yes, yes! The existence of the Gauguin was known, and it was covered with a replica of itself. But nobody knew until now that Gauguin himself had been hired by Gobseck to cover the *St. Stephen*. Here is a letter to prove it. It was written in Paris after Gauguin's last exhibition there in 1893, at Durand–Ruel's. To old Camille Pissarro, who wanted money. Look!"

It was a rambling letter, written in that violet ink which, with the pinpoint pen–nib, used to be at the service of the patrons of most French cafés. It was a very good letter — the man I paid to write it could copy a $20 bill line–for–line in five hours with pen and brush. The cogent passage, freely translated, ran:

> *The exhibition at Durand–Ruel was a bloody fiasco, a catastrophe. Bah! To the critics I say, "Shut your mausoleums, you penny–a–liners — the bones stink!" As for money, what does one use for it? How I hate Paris and the Parisians! I earned myself a species of dishonest penny the other day, and oh my friend, the irony of it!*
>
> *That bloated swine of a Lucien Gobseck got hold of a daub by that maudlin skeleton–man El Greco, of the Stoning of St. Stephen — stolen, of course, from the Kuwalsky–Brzesky mansion. And for 1500 francs I was commissioned secretly to paint "something of my own, just anything" over it.*
>
> *I must admit that it gave me a certain pleasure to smother one of Theotocopouli's maudlin Saints. And so my dreamy Oalámaóa's pagan nudity smothers the Cretan priest's boy's sheet–tin–draped, angular, tubercular visions. There is a melancholy satisfaction in this ...*

"It breathes the very spirit of Gauguin," I said; and I should have known, for I composed it myself. "It was for a long time among Pissarro's papers. Nobody seemed to know what Gauguin was talking about. But now we know. And here is the point — no El Greco is listed in the Gobseck inventory, so Imogene Gribble will be free to sell in the open market. Three hundred thousand dollars would not be too much for a new El Greco!"

"You did right to come to me first with this letter," said Mollock. "I take it as an act of good faith. I hold you entirely innocent in that other unfortunate affair. Let's talk about this ..."

He plied me with wine, he charmed me, he put the matter in a kaleidoscope of different colors and a conjurer's cabinet of angles — and at last he got that letter out of me for $5000 down and a verbal promise of "a percentage of assessed values to be mutually agreed upon."

And after that, I suppose, he went to work on Dreidl: it must have been like an apache dance of mud-wrestlers. I simply disappeared. If anybody ever scraped the third *Oalámaóa* off that tormented canvas, I can tell you what they found: an execrably daubed *Cupid and Psyche*, painter unknown, dated 1610.

"What happened to Molosso and his wife?" I asked, as Karmesin casually pocketed my cigarettes.

"The inevitable. As soon as I paid him his ninety thousand dollars he ran away with a big blonde. I had saved ten thousand for his wife. She divorced him and married a man who has a restaurant at Nogent-sur-Marne. She is happy, and has two children. Molosso had to marry the big blonde, who beats him unmercifully whenever he misbehaves. My mission was accomplished."

"And Mollock was the main victim, really?"

"Yes. He was not a gentleman. He wounded my sensibilities. He tried to bribe and corrupt me," said Karmesin. "Still, all weighed and paid, I suppose I cleared about two hundred thousand dollars, give or take a thousand."

And, having emptied the sugar bowl, he rose and left the café.

The Karmesin Affair

On a blast of bitter east wind that rushed down Great Russell Street came a spatter of cold raindrops that bit like small shot. I reached the portico of the British Museum one jump ahead of the storm, and there, standing apart from the students who had come out of the reading room for air and sandwiches, illuminated by a lightning flash, stood Karmesin in a black rubber Inverness cape reaching to his ankles and an oilskin hat shaped like a gloxinia.

One hand grasped a Kaffir knobkerrie with a gold-plated head, while the other applied motions as of artificial respiration to his half drowned moustache, and he was glaring at a Polynesian monolith in such a manner that I half expected its great stone eyes to look uneasily away.

"Third storm this morning," I said.

He looked at me, glowering like the Spirit of the Tempest.

"A wretched day would not be complete without you. I would invite you to offer me coffee, if I did not object to sitting at table with imbeciles," he muttered. "Do you realize I could sue you, your publishers and printers, your distributors, news agents and booksellers for millions? And I would, too, if I needed petty cash. How dare you describe me as 'either the greatest criminal or the greatest liar the world has ever known'? This is libelous: a liar always betrays a desire to be believed. Damn your impudence, have I ever cared whether you believed me or not?"

"No," I said, "but —"

"No," he interrupted. "And you assume that a truly great criminal never talks of his work, but how wrong you are! A confession unsupported by evidence is only a story, you suppose — and I leave no evidence. I run no risk in telling you certain incidents, you scribbler, to enable you to put a few greasy pennies in your moth-eaten pockets. Remember this: the most pitiful sucker on earth is your skeptic. If you insist, we will go to the Cheese Restaurant and have a bit of Brie and a glass of wine, if you can pay."

The rain abating, we went; but Karmesin was not easily to be placated this morning. He continued, "It's not so much your catchphrases that annoy me as your writing. I read your version of how, having disguised myself as a statue in Westminster Abbey, I discovered a sonnet of Shakespeare in Spenser's tomb, and I blushed for you."

"All I did was —" I began, but Karmesin interjected, "You be quiet!" At least the cheese appeared to please him. "I like Brie and wine," he said.

"They are the two things in this world that are impossible to fake. Not even Melmoth Agnew could successfully counterfeit their flavor."

"Strange name," I said.

"Strange man," said Karmesin. "If only you could write, what a story you might tell about him and me — for without me, he is nothing — and about the Society for the Clarification of History." He shook his great head. "But I can just see you describing Melmoth Agnew, for instance, as 'an anaglyphic character' — here you put three dots — 'a personality in low relief' — then more dots — 'in other words, he had practically no individuality of his own.'"

I said, "Have more cheese. For goodness' sake, have some more wine. Have a cigarette."

He accepted gruffly and continued, "I had occasion just now to upbraid a certain inky little penny–a–liner not a hundred miles from here in connection with a sonnet of Shakespeare. Then, the name of Melmoth Agnew comes up in connection with cheese, and in spite of myself I find myself telling you that I once employed the fellow in a matter concerning quite a different kind of Shakespearean document."

I said, "What sort of document?"

"Ah, you are saying to yourself, 'Old Karmesin is going to tell me now that he discovered a lost play by that greatest of poets.' As usual, you are entirely wrong," he said, then told this story:

I employed Agnew when I felt morally bound to do a service for a distressed gentleman. Do you know what a gentleman is? A gentleman is one who, among other things does not twist his friends' conversation into excruciating prose forms and hawk them from editor to editor (said Karmesin, giving hard look).

The gentleman we will call Sir Massey Joyce, of King's Massey, in Kent. I had not seen him for a long time; nobody had. They said he had turned recluse and buried himself in the country. Having been abroad for some years I had lost touch with him.

Then, one day, certain business taking me to Ashford, it occurred to me to drive over and say "How d'you do."

You have seen photographs of King's Massey in *Stately Homes of England*. It is a beautiful old house, in three different styles of architecture — early Tudor, part of it "modernized" by Inigo Jones in the 1620's, with a wing by Adam built in the Eighteenth Century — the incongruities oddly harmonious.

Massey Joyce was confused, almost embarrassed. He said, "My dear fellow, come in! Come in!"

For a recluse, I thought, he was remarkably pleased to have company. "It's nearly dinnertime," Massey said. "Let's have a glass of sherry," and the old butler, Hubbard, served us, while my host chattered of things past in London.

He is lonely, I said to myself as we went in to dinner. The great mahogany table was set sumptuously with the Joyce plate. The huge silver–gilt centerpiece was heaped with fresh fruit. Old Hubbard poured us a rare old Chablis and served a fish course — three tinned sardines.

After this the entree came up: vegetables and, on a gleaming silver platter, canned corned beef, thinly sliced. With this — well, did you ever try bully beef with a vintage *Clos–Vougeot?* It's rather curious.

And then there was a little block of pasteurized synthetic cheese with a bottle of rare old port, and some coffee–type essence in cups of Sevres porcelain accompanied by a hundred–year–old brandy and superlative cigars.

After dinner, sitting over more brandy in the library, Massey Joyce said to me, "There's enough wine and cigars in the cellar and the cabinets to last out my time: I don't entertain much nowadays. But for the rest, one rubs along, what?"

I said, "It might appear, old friend, that things aren't all they should be."

He answered, "Confidentially, I'm stone broke. I say nothing of taxes. Certain domestic affairs, which we'll not discuss, set me back more than I had — over a quarter of a million. Everything you see, except the wine, the tobacco and these books, is entailed or mortgaged."

I said, "I know, Massey. Norway sardines and Argentine beef might be a quirk of taste; but never penny paraffin candles in silver–gilt sconces."

"Well, I can't bilk the fishmonger and the butcher," said he. "The books must go next."

I was shocked at this. Sir Massey Joyce's library was his haven, his last refuge. It was not that he was a bibliophile: He loved his library — the very presence of all those ranged volumes with their fine scent of old leather comforted him and soothed his soul.

He went on, "Anyway, this is a deuced expensive room to heat. I'll save insurance too. I'll read in the little study, where it's snug. Oh, I know what's in your mind, old boy. How much do I need, and all that, eh? Well, to see my way out with a clear conscience, I want ten thousand pounds. Borrowing is out of the question — I could never pay back."

I said, "Between old friends, Massey, is there nothing I can do for you?"

"Stay with me a day or two. There's a man coming about the library. I thought I might get more, selling by private treaty. He isn't a dealer; he's an agent for the Society for the Clarification of History. You know, ever since Boswell's diary was found in an old trunk, there's hardly an attic or a private collection in England they haven't pawed over. I'm told they have all the money in the world, and anything they want they'll pay a fancy price for. What the devil *is* this Society for the Clarification of History, anyway?"

I said, "You know how it is — a few people like to make something, but most people prefer to break something. You may earn a crust for praising great men, but you will get rich belittling them. The Society for the Clarification of History is fundamentally a debunking society; it's just the kind of thing fidgety millionaires' widows like to play with.

"It's back–fence gossip on a cosmic scale. There's excitement in it and controversy in it and publicity; and it's less bourgeois than endowing orphanages — and not half as expensive. They like to prove all kinds of things — they are heritage busters and tradition wreckers: Paul Revere couldn't ride; Daniel Boone was a Bohun and, therefore, rightful king of England; the author of Othello, in certain lines addressed by the Moor to

Iago, prophesied the great Fire of Chicago. Touching which, their great ambition is to prove beyond doubt that Francis Bacon wrote the works of William Shakespeare. They'd give their eyeteeth for incontrovertible evidence of that."

"All poppycock!" Massey Joyce shouted. "Bacon did nothing of the sort."

"I know he didn't. But why do you want me to stay?"

"I beg pardon, old fellow. That Baconian nonsense always irritates me. Apart from the joy it is to have you here, I want you with me because one of these Clarification of History people called Dr. Olaf Brod is coming Wednesday morning. You're shrewd. I'm not. Handle the business for me?"

I said I would and that he was not to worry; but my heart misgave me. True, Massey Joyce had 25,000 volumes, many of them rare, especially in the category of the drama. But books, when you want to buy them, are costly, and when you need to sell them, valueless. However much had been spent on the library, Massey Joyce would be very lucky to get a couple of thousand pounds for the lot.

I did not sleep well that night; the owls kept hooting O *Iago!* ... *Iago* ... *Iago* ...

I was concerned for my old friend; in times like these, we must preserve such honorable anachronisms as Sir Massey Joyce. He was the last of a fine old breed: a benevolent landlord, proud but sweet-natured, and a great sportsman.

He was the Horseman of the Shires, who had finished the course in the Grand National; at the Amateurs' Club he had fought eight rounds with Bob Fitzsimmons; as a cricketer he was one of the finest batsmen in the country; and he was a stubborn defender of individual liberty, a protector of the poor, and third-best-dressed man in England. A Complete Man.

And, furthermore, a patron of the arts, especially of the theatre — his first wife was Delia Yorke, a fine comic actress and a very beautiful woman in her day.

This marriage was perfectly happy. Delia was the good angel of the countryside. But they had a wretch of a son, and he went to the dogs — he drank, swindled, forged, embezzled and, to hush matters up, Massey Joyce paid. Having run down to the bottom of the gamut of larceny, the young scoundrel became a gossip columnist and then went out in a blaze of scandal, when a woman he was trying to blackmail shot him. This broke Delia's heart, and she died a year later.

But my dear friend Massey Joyce had to live on, and so he did, putting a brave front on it. Then he married again, because he met a girl who reminded him of his truly beloved Delia. She was much younger than Massey, also an actress, and her only resemblance to Delia was in her manner of speaking: she had studied it, of course. This was the best job of acting that shallow little performer ever did.

Massey financed three plays for her. They were complete failures. She blamed Massey naturally, left him, and ran off with a Romanian film director.

Massey let her divorce him, saying, "That Romanian won't last. Poor Alicia can't act, and she ain't the kind of beauty that mellows with age. She'll need to eat. It's my fault anyway. What business has an old man marrying a young woman? Serves me right."

Outwardly he looked the same, but he seemed to have lost interest. He sold his stable, rented his shooting, stopped coming up to town for the first nights, sold his house in Manchester Square, resigned from his clubs, locked up most of King's Massey, and lived as I have described. I had not known he was so poor.

Before dawn, giving up all hope of sleep, I carried my candle down to the library: the electricity had been cut off, of course.

A glance at the catalogue more than confirmed my misgivings. Readers of these kinds of books are becoming fewer and fewer; there was not a dealer in the country who would trouble to give Massey Joyce's treasures shelf space.

Hoping against hope, I opened a cabinet marked MSS: ELIZABETHAN. The drawers were full of trivial stuff, mostly contemporary fair copies, so-called, of plays and masques, written by clerks for the use of such leading actors as knew how to read.

My heart grew heavier and heavier. All this stuff was next door to worthless. The sun rose. Chicago, Chicago, Chicago! said a sparrow. And then I had an idea.

I took out of the cabinet a tattered old promptbook of the tragedy of *Hamlet*, copied about 1614 and full of queer abbreviations and misspellings, and carried it up to my room. Although I knew the play by heart, I reread it with minute attention, then put the manuscript in my suitcase, and went down to breakfast.

Over this meal I said to Massey Joyce, "It's understood, now. I have a free hand to deal with this Dr. Olaf Brod and his Society for the Clarification of History?"

"Perfectly," he said. "I'm grateful. He might come out with some of that damned Baconian stuff, and I'd lose my temper."

"Just keep quiet," I said.

And it was as well that Massey Joyce did as I advised, for Olaf Brod was one of those melancholy Danes who rejoice only in being contradictory. His manner was curt and bristly, like his hair.

He bustled in about lunchtime and said, in a peremptory voice, "I haf time now only for a cursory glance. I must go unexpectedly to Wales. Proof positif has been discovert at last of the nonexistence of King Artur. Today is the second of July. I return on der tventiet."

He rushed about the library. "I had been toldt of manuscripts," he said.

I replied, "Doctor, we had better leave those until you can study them."

"Yes," he said, "it is better soh." But he stopped for a quick luncheon. Massey had up some golden glory in the form of an old champagne. Doctor Brod was severe. "I am a vechetarian," he said.

Massey asked, "Isn't wine a vegetable drink, sir?"

With his mouth full of carrots, Brod replied, "Not soh! Dat bottle is a grafeyard. Effery sip you takes contains de putrefiedt corpses of a trillion bacteria of pfermentation."

"Hubbard, fresh water to Doctor Brod," said Massey, but Brod said, "Der water here is full of chalk; it is poisonous. It makes stones in der kidleys."

Massey said, "Been drinking it sixty-five years, and I have no stones in my kidneys, sir."

Olaf Brod answered, "Vait and see. Also, der cigar you schmoke is crematorium of stinking cherms and viruses." Luckily he was in a hurry to leave. But he paused on the threshold to say, "On de tventiet I come again. No more cigars, no more vine, eh? Soh! Boil der vater to precipitade de calcium. Farevell!"

I said to Massey Joyce, having calmed him down, "I'll be here on the nineteenth, old fellow."

He said, "There'll be murder done if you ain't!"

Then I hurried back to town, taking that old promptbook copy of *Hamlet* with me. I also took a little lead from one of the old gutters in the Tudor part of King's Massey.

What for? To make a pencil with, of course; and this was a matter of an hour. I simply rubbed the sliver of metal to as fine a point as it would conveniently take: it wrote dull gray. This done, I went to see Agnew.

You would have loved to describe him; you would have pulled out all the stops (said Karmesin, and in a horrible mockery of my voice and style, he proceeded to improvise). Melmoth had pale, smooth cheeks. His large round eyes, shiny, protuberant, and vague, were like bubbles full of smoke. The merest hint of a cinnamon–brown moustache emphasized the indecision of his upper lip.

He carried his cigarette in a surreptitious way, hidden in a cupped hand. He had something of the air of a boy who has recently been at the doughnuts and is making matters worse by smoking. I half expected his black–silk suit to give out a faint metallic crackle, like burnt paper cooling.

His silk Shantung shirt was of the tints of dust and twilight, and his dull red tie had an ashen bloom on it like that of a dying ember ... That's your kind of writing, give or take a few "ineluctables" and "indescribables" and whatnot. Bah!

Agnew was a kind of sensitized Nobody. You have heard of that blind and witless pianist whom P. T. Barnum exhibited? The one who had only to hear a piece of music played once, and he could play it again, exactly reproducing the touch and the manner of the person who had played before him, whether that person was a music teacher in a kindergarten or a Franz Liszt? Great executants deliberately made tiny mistakes in playing the most complicated fugues; Blind Tom, or whatever they called him, reproduced these errors too.

Agnew was like that, only his talent was with the pen. He had only to look at a holograph, to reproduce it in such a manner that no two handwriting experts could ever agree as to its complete authenticity.

I had previously found several uses for Melmoth Agnew; this time I carried him off to the British Museum, where I made him study some manuscripts of Francis Bacon. This peculiar fellow simply had, in a manner of speaking, to click open the shutters of his eyes and expose himself for a few minutes to what he was told to memorize.

I warned him to take especial care, but he assured me in the most vapid drawl that ever man carried away from Oxford, "The holograph of Lord Verulam, Viscount St. Albans, is indelibly imprinted on my memory, sir. I am ready to transcribe in his calligraphy any document you place before me. Problems of ink, and so on, I leave to you."

"It is to be written with a lead point."

"Then it is child's play," said he, wanly smiling, "but it would be so much nicer in ink."

I knew all about that. There are other experts who, with chemicals and spectroscopes and microscopes, could make child's play of detecting new from old, especially in mixtures like ink and the abrasions made by pens.

Against a coming emergency, which I was anticipating, I had in preparation an ink of copperas, or ferrous sulfate, which I made with unrefined sulfuric acid and iron pyrites; gum arabic out of the binding of a half-gutted Spanish edition of Lactantius dated 1611; and the excrescenses raised by the cynips insect on the *Quercus infestoria*, better known as nutgalls — the whole adulterated with real Elizabethan soot out of one of the blocked-up chimneys of King's Massey. But it would take a year to age this blend, and there was no time to spare. This was none of Agnew's business.

I showed him the promptbook copy of *Hamlet* and said, "Observe that the last half page is blank. Take that lead stylus and, precisely in Francis Bacon's hand, copy me this." I gave him a sheet of paper.

Having perused what I had written there, he said, "I beg pardon, but am I supposed to make sense of this?"

I told him, "No. You are to make a hundred pounds out of it."

So Agnew nodded in slow motion and went to work, silent, in curious, perfect as a fine machine, and the calligraphy of Francis Bacon lived again. He was finished in an hour.

"I'm afraid it's rather pale," he said apologetically.

I said, "I know. Forget it."

And such was his nature that I believe he forgot the matter forthwith; he even had to make an effort to remember his hundred pounds — I had to remind him.

Now I will write out for you, in modern English, what I had given Agnew to copy. In this version I will make certain modifications in spelling so that the riddle I propounded conforms with the key to it. Here:

I seek in vain the Middle Sea to see,
Without it I am not, yet here I be
Lost, in a desperate Soliloquy.
If you would learn this humble name of mine
Take 3 and 16 and a score–and–9.
Count 30, 31, and 46,
Be sure your ciphers in their order mix,
Thus, after 46 comes 47
As surely as a sinner hopes for Heaven.
Take 56, and 64 and 5,
And so you will by diligence arrive
At numbers 69 and 72.
Five figures running now must wait on you
As 86, 7, 8, 9, ten fall due,
'Tis nearly done. Now do not hesitate.
To mark 100; 56, 7, 8,
My mask is dropt, my little game is o'er
And having read my name, you read no more.

Of course, this should not tax the intelligence of the average coal heaver, in possession of all the clues I have given. Yet, for you, I had better explain!

What desperate Soliloquy in *Hamlet* contains the words, "No more"? The familiar one, of course: "To be, or not to be," and so on.

Examine that somber opening to Hamlet's Soliloquy; and you will notice that, curiously enough, the letter *C* does not occur anywhere in the first six lines. The writer is not a homesick Spaniard or Italian far from the Mediterranean, which formerly was called the "Middle Sea." He refers to the missing *C* in his name. He has buried his identity in the first half dozen lines of Hamlet's familiar Soliloquy.

Having guessed this far — why, babes in kindergarten solve trickier puzzles than this riddle of the rhyming numbers. Starting with "To be," count the letters by their numbers, as far as "No more." Letters *3, 16, 29, 30, 31, 46, 47, 56, 64, 65, 69, 72, 86, 87, 88, 89, 90, 156, 157* and *158*. So it reads:

To Be, or not to be — thAt is the questiON:
Whether 'tis nobleR In the mind To suffer
THe slIngS and arrows of ouTRAGEous fortune
Or to take arms against a sea of troubles,
And by opposing end them. To DIE — to sleep
No more ...

Hence, "Ba-on writ this tragedie." Without his middle C, Bacon is not; yet here he is. And so he tells you — and in his own handwriting too!

A real lawyer's split–hair quibble, what? Just tortuous enough. A meaty bone for the debunkers, eh? It might be asked, "Why should Bacon have written this?" The answer is: "Bacon liked actors; he wrote it in a promptbook to amuse some sprightly player after a theatrical supper, circa 1615."

So, having suitably oxidized the faint lead in the pencil marks, half erasing them in a process of ever so gently abrasion, I returned to King's Massey on the nineteenth and slipped the promptbook back where I had found it.

Massey Joyce said, "I do hope this Brod man coughs up. Do you know, Hubbard and his wife — who cooks and housekeeps — haven't had any wages for three years? I tried to pay 'em off when I sold my guns and sporting prints, but they wouldn't go. Begged pardon; said they'd known the good times, and by the Lord Harry they'd stand by in the bad."

"Do those Elizabethan manuscripts of yours mean much to you?" I asked.

He said, "No. Why?"

I told him, "Why then, Massey, we'll save your old books yet. Only you keep out of it. Have a migraine; keep to your room and leave it to me."

So he did: and Doctor Brod turned up on the morning of the twentieth with a friend, one Doctor Brewster, also of the Society for the Clarification of History, but lean and keen, with a businesslike dry-cleaned look about him. As I had expected, they found little enough to interest them on the bookshelves.

By the time they got to the manuscripts Brod was already fidgeting and looking at his watch. Casually forcing my marked promptbook on them, somewhat as a conjurer does when he makes you pick a card, I said, "I doubt if there's much here. But Sir Massey regards these holographs as the apple of his eye. The one you have there is rather defaced, I'm afraid. A lot of the others are in much better condition."

But Brod, suddenly perspiring like a pressed duckling, had a reading glass out, and Brewster was putting on a pair of microscope spectacles, and they were scrutinizing my little poem in the strong sunlight by the window.

Brod took out notebook and pencil and made voluminous notes, occasionally nudging Brewster, who remained blank and impassive. *They* knew Bacon's hand, bless their hearts! And cryptograms were meat and drink to the likes of them.

After a while, with complete composure, Brewster said, "I don't know. It's possible the Society might be interested in two or three of these manuscripts."

But I said, "I'm awfully sorry; two or three won't do, I'm afraid. Sir Massey regards this collection as a whole. He'd never break it up. There are interesting fragments by Nathaniel Field, for example, and Middleton, and Fletcher. I'm no expert, Doctor, only a friendly agent."

"Sir Massey Joyce would not refuse permission to photograph or copy certain excerpts," said Brod

I answered, "I'm afraid he would."

Then Brewster asked, "Has this collection ever been offered for sale before?"

I told him, "Never. It has never been properly catalogued, I'm afraid."

Brewster tossed the *Hamlet* nonchalantly, as if it were a mail-order catalogue, onto a baize-covered table — I wouldn't advise a novice to play poker with that one — and he asked, "How much is Massey Joyce asking for the collection?"

Apologizing, as for an embarrassing but harmless eccentric, I said, "Well, you see, Sir Massey values things strictly in proportion to how much he personally likes them. So he swears he won't sell manuscripts for a penny less than twenty-five thousand pounds."

I laughed here, and so did Doctor Brewster, while Brod muttered something about "vine drunkards" and "devourers of the charred carcasses of slaughtered beasts."

I put the *Hamlet* back in its drawer and continued, "I know it's absurd; but when a man of Sir Massey's age has an *idée fixe* — you know? I'm afraid I've wasted your time. Well, I suppose you can't find some thing in your line every time you look. Oh, by the way, do you happen to know a collector named Lilienbach? He's coming next Monday. I wondered if he was all right."

I knew, of course, that Doctor Lilienbach of Philadelphia was one of the richest collectors of rare books and manuscripts in the world; and, of course, these fellows were sure to know this too.

"Lilienbach," Brod began, but Brewster cut in, "Lilienbach, Lilienbach? No, I can't say I know him. Let's not be hasty. These things take time. Look here; say I pay Sir Massey Joyce a small sum down for an option to purchase on terms to be mutually agreed?"

I said, "I shouldn't, if I were you — not until Sir Massey has had a chance to talk to Doctor Lilienbach."

Then there was a silence until, at last, Brewster said, "I'll have to call Chicago. Even if I were interested, I couldn't make any sort of bid before tonight."

I said, "Why not do that? Only I'm afraid you'll have to call from Ashford, Sir Massey does not believe in telephones. He thinks they cause rheumatism."

And to cut a long story short: after a day of negotiation the Society for the Clarification of History authorized Brewster to purchase Sir Massey Joyce's Elizabethan manuscripts, with all rights pertaining thereto, for £17,500.

So my old friend kept his books and had some money to support himself and the Hubbards in their declining years.

Karmesin paused. I asked, "And you got nothing?"

Karmesin said, "Massey Joyce wanted me to take half. I couldn't possibly, of course. Am I a petty larcenist to work for chicken feed? No. My amusements are few; I had my fun. For a small outlay, I had the double-barreled pleasure of helping a friend in need at the expense of an organization which I despise."

There being a wedge of cheese left, Karmesin wrapped it in a paper napkin and put it in his pocket.

I said, "I've read nothing of your 'Baconian' document as yet."

"You will. They are preparing a book about it, and my ink is brewing for a counterblast that will shake the world. You just wait and see!"

"So there the matter ended?"

Karmesin grunted, "After dinner that night Massey Joyce said to me, 'It is astounding that such societies can exist. They really believe Bacon wrote Shakespeare! No, really, there are limits! Was ever a more pernicious fable hatched by cranks?' "

" 'Never,' I said.

" 'It is wonderful what people can be gulled into believing — Bacon, indeed! Why, every shopgirl knows that the plays of William Shakespeare, so-called, were written by Christopher Marlowe!' said Massey Joyce."

Karmesin Bibliography

"Karmesin"
    Evening Standard, May 9 1936
    Best Stories of the Underworld (ed. Peter Cheyney, Faber & Faber 1942)
    The People, April 2, 1944, as "Karmesin!"
    Ellery Queen's Mystery Magazine (US), April 1948, as "Karmesin, Bank Robber"
    Argosy (UK), December 1949
    Everybody's, August 17, 1957, as "A Slight Miscalculation"

"Karmesin and the Meter"
    Courier, Winter 1937/38
    The People, November 26, 1944
    Ellery Queen's Mystery Magazine (US), December 1947, as "Karmesin, Swindler"
    Courier, January 1948
    Argosy (UK), August 1950, as "Karmesin and the Big Frost"
    Ellery Queen's 1961 Anthology (ed. Ellery Queen, Davis 1960), as "Karmesin, Swindler"
    Ellery Queen's Minimysteries (ed. Ellery Queen, World 1969), as "Karmesin, Swindler"

"Karmesin and Human Vanity"
    Courier, Spring 1938
    The People, December 10, 1944
    Ellery Queen's Mystery Magazine (US), May 1949, as "Karmesin, Con Man"
    Argosy (UK), May 1950

"Karmesin and the Tailor's Dummy"
    Courier, Autumn 1938
    Ellery Queen's Mystery Magazine (US), December 1947, as "Karmesin, Criminal Lawyer"

Argosy (UK), July 1950

"Karmesin and the Big Flea"
Courier, Winter 1938/39
Ellery Queen's Mystery Magazine (US), July 1949, as "Karmesin, Blackmailer"
Lilliput, May 1954, as "Karmesin Beats the Blackmailers"

"Karmesin and the Raving Lunatic"
Courier, Spring 1939
Best Stories of the Underworld (ed. Peter Cheyney, Faber & Faber, 1942)
Ellery Queen's Mystery Magazine (US), November 1945, as "Karmesin, Jewel Thief"
Mystère Magazine 24, January 1950, as "Karmesin Voleur de Bijoux"
Argosy (UK), February 1950, as "A Bracelet for Karmesin"
Lilliput, July 1954, as "Karmesin and the Man Who Was Mad About Diamonds"
Everybody's, November 2, 1957, as "Bracelet For A Man Of Genius"
Courier, November 1958

"Karmesin and the Unbeliever"
Courier, Summer 1939
The People, January 7, 1945
Argosy (UK), June 1950
Ellery Queen's Mystery Magazine (US), August 1950, as "Karmesin, Racketeer"

"Inscrutable Providence"
The People, December 24, 1944
Ellery Queen's Mystery Magazine (US), November 1945, as "Karmesin, Murderer"
Mystère Magazine 24, January 1950, as "Karmesin Meurtrier"
London After Midnight (ed. Peter Haining, Little, Brown 1996, Warner 1997), as "Karmesin the Murderer"

"Karmesin and the Invisible Millionaire"
Courier, Winter 1945
Ellery Queen's Mystery Magazine (US), March 1969, as "Karmesin and the Trismagistus Formula"
Mystère Magazine 258, August 1969, as "Karmesin et la Formule de

Karmesin Bibliography

Trismagistus" (trans. by French Denise Baye)

"Karmesin and the Gorgeous Robes"
Courier, May 1946

"Chickenfeed for Karmesin"
Courier, December 1946
Courier, November 1962
Ellery Queen's Mystery Magazine (US), January 1970, as "Karmesin the Fixer"
Mystère Magazine 281, July 1971, as "L'Intermédiaire" (trans. into French by M. Kinsky)

"The Thief Who Played Dead"
Saturday Evening Post, February 13, 1954
John Bull, May 22, 1954, as "A Tomb for Karmesin"
New Zealand Herald, July 24, 1954
The Ugly Face of Love by Gerald Kersh (Heinemann, 1960, Ace H534, 1962), as "Collector's Piece"
Ellery Queen's Mystery Magazine (US), July 1960
Ellery Queen's Mystery Magazine (UK), September 1960
Mystère Magazine 156, January 1961, as "Le Voleur Qui Fit le Mort" (trans. into French by Arlette Rosenblum)
Ellery Queen's 1969 Anthology (ed. Ellery Queen, Davis 1969)

"The Conscience of Karmesin"
Lilliput, April 1954
Argosy (US), July 1954 as "The Impossible Robbery"
Ellery Queen's Mystery Magazine (US), Feb 1959, as "Karmesin and the Crown Jewels"
Mystère Magazine 164, September 1961, as "Karmesin et les Joyeaux de la Couronne" (trans. into French by Roger Guerbet)
Ellery Queen's Anthology 1966 Mid-Year Edition (ed. Ellery Queen, Davis, 1966), as "Karmesin and the Crown Jewels"

"Karmesin and the Royalties"
Courier, January 1956
Argosy (US), date unknown, as "Karmesin and the Publisher"
Ellery Queen's Mystery Magazine (US), November 1964, as "Karmesin Takes Pen in Hand"

Ellery Queen's Anthology, Fall–Winter 1971 (ed. Ellery Queen, Davis, 1971), as "Karmesin Takes Pen in Hand"

"Skate's Eyeball"
Argosy (UK), April 1960
Argosy (US), date unknown
Ellery Queen's Mystery Magazine (US), August 1964, as "Honor Among Thieves"
Mystère Magazine 223, August 1968, as "Les Loups Entre Eux" (trans. into French by Arlette Rosenblum)
Ellery Queen's 1971 Anthology (ed. Ellery Queen, Davis, 1970), as "Honor Among Thieves"
Anthologie Mystère Magazine 16 (249b) 1972, as "L'Honneur du Milieu" (trans. into French by Robert Berghe)

"Oalámaóa"
Playboy, December 1960
Ellery Queen's Mystery Magazine (US), July 1962, as "A Deal in Overcoats"
Ellery Queen's Mystery Magazine (UK), November 1962, as "A Deal in Overcoats"
Mystère Magazine 179, December 1962, as "Karmesin et le Faux Gauguin" (trans. into French by Catherine Gregoire)
More Than Once Upon A Time by Gerald Kersh (Heinemann 1964), as "The Molosso Overcoats"

"The Karmesin Affair"
Saturday Evening Post, December 15, 1962
The Hospitality of Miss Tolliver by Gerald Kersh (Heinemann 1965), as "Bone For Debunkers"
Ellery Queen's Mystery Magazine (US), Jan 1966, as "Karmesin and the Hamlet Promptbook"
Mystère Magazine 233, June 1967, as "Karmesin Faussaire et Philantrope" (trans. into French by Jean Laustenne)
Nightshade & Damnations (ed. Harlan Ellison, Gold Medal R1887, 1968; Coronet 0839, 1969), as "Bone for Debunkers"

Karmesin Bibliography

FURTHER READING:

Fowlers End by Gerald Kersh, introduction by Michael Moorcock, Harvill Press (UK)
Night and the City by Gerald Kersh, introduction by Paul Duncan, ibooks
The Nights and Cities of Gerald Kersh – www.harlanellison.com/kersh – run by Paul Duncan
Kersh Chat Room — http://clubs.yahoo.com/clubs/geraldkersh — run by Jeff Wood

ABOUT THE EDITOR

Paul Duncan has been researching Gerald Kersh for over ten years and is preparing a biography for publication. You can contact him at kershed@aol.com - he is always happy to hear from people around the world who can add to his bibliography. Paul has written about noir fiction and film for Pocket Essentials (www.pocketessentials.com) and is currently editing film books for Taschen (www.taschen.com).

Karmesin: The World's Greatest Criminal — Or Most Outrageous Liar

Karmesin: The World's Greatest Criminal — Or Most Outrageous Liar by Gerald Kersh is set in 12-point Garamond font and printed on 60 pound natural shade opaque acid-free paper. The cover painting is by Carol Heyer and the Lost Classics design is by Deborah Miller. *Karmesin: The World's Greatest Criminal — Or Most Outrageous Liar* was published in June 2003 by Crippen & Landru, Publishers, Norfolk, Virginia.

CRIPPEN & LANDRU, PUBLISHERS
P. O. Box 9315
Norfolk, VA 23505
E-mail: info@crippenlandru.com
www.crippenlandru.com

Crippen & Landru publishes first editions of short-story collections by important detective and mystery writers.

☞This is the best edited, most attractively packaged line of mystery books introduced in this decade. The books are equally valuable to collectors and readers. [*Mystery Scene Magazine*]

☞The specialty publisher with the most star-studded list is Crippen & Landru, which has produced short story collections by some of the biggest names in contemporary crime fiction. [*Ellery Queen's Mystery Magazine*]

☞God Bless Crippen & Landru. [*The Strand Magazine*]

☞A monument in the making is appearing year by year from Crippen & Landru, a small press devoted exclusively to publishing the criminous short story. [*Alfred Hitchcock's Mystery Magazine*]

Crippen & Landru is proud to publish a series of *new* short-story collections by great authors of the past who specialized in traditional mysteries. Each book collects stories from crumbling pages of old pulp, digest, and slick magazines, and most of the stories have been "lost" since their first publication. The following books are in print:

The Newtonian Egg and Other Cases of Rolf le Roux by Peter Godfrey, introduction by Ronald Godfrey. 2002. Trade softcover, $15.00.

Murder, Mystery and Malone by Craig Rice, edited by Jeffrey A. Marks. 2002. Trade softcover, $19.00.

The Sleuth of Baghdad: The Inspector Chafik Stories, by Charles B. Child. Cloth, $27.00. 2002. Trade softcover, $17.00.

Hildegarde Withers: Uncollected Riddles by Stuart Palmer, introduction by Mrs. Stuart Palmer. 2002. Trade softcover, $19.00.

The Spotted Cat and Other Mysteries from the Casebook of Inspector Cockrill by Christianna Brand, edited by Tony Medawar. 2002. Cloth, $29.00. Trade softcover, $19.00.

Marksman and Other Stories by William Campbell Gault, edited by Bill Pronzini; afterword by Shelley Gault. 2003. Trade softcover, $19.00.

Karmesin: The World's Greatest Criminal — Or Most Outrageous Liar by Gerald Kersh, edited by Paul Duncan. 2003. Cloth, $27.00. Trade softcover, $17.00.

The Complete Curious Mr. Tarrant by C. Daly King, introduction by Edward D. Hoch. 2003. Cloth, $29.00. Trade softcover, $19.00.

2003. Cloth, $27.00. Trade softcover, $18.00.

Murder – All Kinds by William L. DeAndrea, introduction by Jane Haddam. 2003. Cloth, $29.00. Trade softcover, $19.00.

The Avenging Chance and Other Mysteries from Roger Sheringham's Casebook by Anthony Berkeley, edited by Tony Medawar and Arthur Robinson. 2004. Cloth, $29.00. Trade softcover, $19.00.

Banner Deadlines: The Impossible Files of Senator Brooks U. Banner by Joseph Commings, edited by Robert Adey; memoir by Edward D. Hoch. 2004. Cloth, $29.00. Trade softcover, $19.00.

The Danger Zone and Other Stories by Erle Stanley Gardner, edited by Bill Pronzini. 2004. Cloth, $29.00. Trade softcover, $19.00.

Dr. Poggioli: Criminologist by T. S. Stribling, edited by Arthur Vidro. Cloth, $29.00. 2004. Trade softcover, $19.00.

The Couple Next Door: Collected Short Mysteries by Margaret Millar, edited by Tom Nolan. 2004. Trade softcover, $19.00.

Sleuth's Alchemy: Cases of Mrs. Bradley and Others by Gladys Mitchell, edited by Nicholas Fuller. 2004. Cloth, $29.00. Trade softcover, $19.00.

Who Was Guilty? Two Dime Novels by Philip S. Warne/Howard W. Macy, edited by Marlena E. Bremseth. 2004. Cloth, $29.00. Trade softcover, $19.00.

Slot-Machine Kelly by Michael Collins, introduction by Robert J. Randisi. Cloth, $29.00. 2004. Trade softcover, $19.00.

The Evidence of the Sword by Rafael Sabatini, edited by Jesse F. Knight. 2006. Cloth, $29.00. Trade softcover, $19.00.

The Casebook of Sidney Zoom by Erle Stanley Gardner, edited by Bill Pronzini. 2006. Cloth, $29.00. Trade softcover, $19.00.

2006. Cloth, $29.00. Trade softcover, $19.00.
The Trinity Cat and Other Mysteries by Ellis Peters (Edith Pargeter), edited by Martin Edwards and Sue Feder. 2006. Trade softcover, $19.00.
The Grandfather Rastin Mysteries by Lloyd Biggle, Jr., edited by Kenneth Lloyd Biggle and Donna Biggle Emerson. 2007. Cloth, $29.00. Trade softcover, $19.00.
Masquerade: Ten Crime Stories by Max Brand, edited by William F. Nolan. 2007. Cloth, $29.00. Trade softcover, $19.00.
Dead Yesterday and Other Mysteries by Mignon G. Eberhart, edited by Rick Cypert and Kirby McCauley. Cloth, $30.00. Trade softcover, $20.00.

FORTHCOMING LOST CLASSICS

The Battles of Jericho by Hugh Pentecost, introduction by S.T. Karnick
The Minerva Club, The Department of Patterns and Other Stories by Victor Canning, edited by John Higgins
The Casebook of Gregory Hood by Anthony Boucher and Denis Green, edited by Joe R. Christopher
Erle Stanley Gardner, *The Exploits of the Patent Leather Kid*, edited by Bill Pronzini.
The Casebook of Jonas P. Jonas and Others by Elizabeth Ferrars, edited by John Cooper
Ten Thousand Blunt Instruments by Philip Wylie, edited by Bill Pronzini.
Erle Stanley Gardner, *The Exploits of the Patent Leather Kid*, edited by Bill Pronzini.
Vincent Cornier, *Duel of Shadows*, edited by Mike Ashley.
Phyllis Bentley, *Author in Search of a Character: The Detections of Miss Phipps*, edited by Marvin Lachman.
Balduin Groller, *Detective Dagobert: Master Sleuth of Old Vienna*, translated by Thomas Riediker.

SUBSCRIPTIONS

Crippen & Landru offers discounts to individuals and institutions who place Standing Order Subscriptions for its forthcoming publications, either all the Regular Series or all the Lost Classics or (preferably) both. Collectors can thereby guarantee receiving limited editions, and readers won't miss any favorite stories. Standing Order Subscribers receive a specially commissioned story in a deluxe edition as a gift at the end of the year. Please write or e-mail for more details.

Printed in the United States
98711LV00005B/169-210/A